D1030554

The Marquise
&
Pauline

OTHER BOOKS BY GEORGE SAND IN
ACADEMY CHICAGO EDITIONS

The Bagpipers

Indiana

The Intimate Journal

Lucrezia Floriani

Mauprat

Valentine

Winter in Majorca

GEORGE SAND

The Marquise
&
Pauline

TRANSLATED BY
Sylvie Charron and Sue Huseman

INTRODUCTION AND NOTES BY
Sylvie Charron

ACADEMY CHICAGO PUBLISHERS

Published in 1999 by
Academy Chicago Publishers
363 West Erie Street
Chicago, Illinois 60610

Library of Congress Cataloging-in-Publication Data

Sand, George, 1804–1876
    [Marquise. English]
    The marquise ; & Pauline / George Sand ; translated by
Sylvie Charron and Sue Huseman ; introduction and notes by
Sylvie Charron.
       p.   cm.
    ISBN 0-89733-449-3
    I. Charron, Sylvie, professor. II. Huseman, Sue. III. Sand,
George, 1804–1876. Pauline. English. IV. Title. V. Title:
Marquise ; and Pauline VI. Title: Pauline.
    PQ2409.M613   1999
    843'.8—dc21   98-19508
                                           CIP

⋆ *Contents* ⋆

• George Sand Chronology •

1804   July 1: Birth at 15 rue Meslée, Paris, to
Maurice Dupin and Sophie-Victoire
Delaborde. Christened Amantine-Lucile
Aurore. Family moves to rue de la
Crande-Batelière, Paris.

1808   Aurore travels to Spain with her mother.
They join her father at the Palace de
Godoy in Madrid where he is serving in
Napoleon's army under General Murat.
The family travels to Nohant in France,
the home of Maurice Dupin's mother,
born Marie-Aurore de Saxe, Comtesse de
Horne, daughter of the illegitimate son of
King Frederick-Augustus II of Poland.
Sept 16: Death of Maurice Dupin, age 30,
in a fall from a horse.

1809   Feb 3: Sophie-Victoire gives custody of
Aurore to Mme Dupin de Francueil, her
mother-in-law, in return for payment of
Maurice's debts and a pension of 1000
francs a year.

1810–1814 Winters in Paris at rue Neuve-des-Mathurins with her grandmother. Visits from Sophie-Victoire. Summers at Nohant.

1818–1820 Educated at the English Convent des Augustines in Paris.

1820 Returns to Nohant. Studies with her father's tutor, Deschartres. Rides horse-back in male clothing.

1821 Death of Mme Dupin de Francueil. Aurore inherits money, a house in Paris and the house at Nohant.

1822 Moves in with her mother at 80 rue St-Lazare, Paris.
April: Meets Casimir-François Dudevant, son of Baron Dudevant, on a visit to the Duplessis family.
September 10: Marries Dudevant. They move to Nohant in October.

1823 June 30: Maurice is born at Hôtel de Florence, 56 rue Neuve-des-Mathurins, Paris.

1824 Spring and summer at the Duplessis' at Plessis-Picard near Melun; autumn at a Parisian suburb, Ormesson; winter in an apartment at rue du Faubourg-St Honoré.

1825 Spring at Nohant. Aurore is ill in the summer. Dudevants travel to his family home in Gascony. Vacation in the

Pyrenees where she meets Aurélian de Sèze and recovers her health.
Nov 5: Writes long letter to Casimir confessing attraction to de Sèze. She gives him up. Winter in Gascony.

1827   Takes Stéphane de Grandsagne as lover. They meet in Paris.

1828   Sept 13: Birth of Solange.

1829   Writes *Voyage en Auvergne,* unpublished in her lifetime. Sees de Sèze.

1830   Visit to de Sèze in Bordeaux. Their correspondence ceases. She writes a novel, *Aimée,* which she later burns. Meets new lover, Jules Sandeau.
Dec: Discovers Casimir's will, filled with antipathy toward her. Decides to separate from him, to spend half the year in Paris, leaving the children in Nohant.

1831   Jan 4: Moves to Paris, to 31 rue de Seine, to live secretly with Sandeau. Joins staff of *Le Figaro.* Writes three short stories: "La Molinara" (in *Figaro*), "La Prima Donna" (in *Revue de Paris*) and "La Fille d'Albano" (in *La Mode*).
April: Returns to Nohant for three months. Writes *Indiana.*
July: Moves to 25 Quai St-Michel, Paris.
Dec: Publishes *Rose et Blanche* in collaboration with Jules Sandeau. Book is signed Jules Sand.

1832   Travel between Paris and Nohant.
April: Brings Solange to Paris. Quarrels
with Sandeau.
May: *Indiana* published.
Nov: Moves to 19 Quai Malaquais with
Solange.
Valentine published. Maurice sent by
Casimir to the Lycée Henri Quatre in
Paris.

1833   Breaks with Sandeau
June: Meets Alfred de Musset.
Publishes *Lélia*.
Sept: To Fontainebleau with Musset.
Dec 10: To Italy with Musset.
Publishes novellas in various journals.

1834   Jan 19: Hotel Danieli in Venice. Musset
attempts a break with Aurore, becomes
ill. His physician is Pietro Pagello.
March 29: Musset returns to Paris.
Aurore remains with Pagello. Publication
of *André, Mattéa, Jacques, Léone Léoni*
and the first *Lettres d'un Voyageur.*
July: Returns to Paris with Pagello.
Aug 24: Musset goes to Baden.
Aug 29: Aurore to Nohant.
Oct: Returns to Paris. Musset returns
from Baden.
Pagello returns to Venice.

Nov 25: Begins journal to de Musset.
Dec: Returns to Nohant.

1835   Jan: Returns to Paris.
Mar 6: Final break with de Musset.
Meets Michel de Bourges, her lawyer and
political mentor.
Writes *Simon.*
Autumn: Returns to Nohant for
Maurice's holiday.
Oct 19: Casimir threatens her physically.
Begins suit for legal separation.
Dec 1: Judgment in her favor won by
default.

1836   Feb 16: She wins second judgment.
Casimir brings suit.
May 10, 11: Another verdict in her favor
from civil court of La Chatre. Casimir
appeals to a higher court.
July 25,26: Trial in royal court of
Bourges. Jury divided. Out-of-court
settlement. Her fortune is divided with
Casimir.
Aug: To Switzerland with Maurice and
Solange, Franz Liszt and Aurore's friend
Marie d'Agoult.
Autumn: Hotel de la France, 15 rue
Lafitte, Paris, with Liszt and d'Agoult.
Meets Chopin.

1837   Jan: Returns to Nohant.
Publishes *Mauprat* in spring. Writes *Les Maîtres Mosaïstes.* Liszt and d'Agoult visit Nohant. Fatal illness of Sophie-Victoire in Paris. Visit to Fontainebleau. Writes *La Dernière Aldini.* Trip to Gascony to recover Solange, who has been kidnapped by Casimir.

1838   Writes *L'Orco* and *L'Uscoque,* two Venetian novels.
May: To Paris. Romance with Chopin. Nov: Trip to Majorca with children and Chopin.
Writes *Spiridion. La Dernière Aldini* published.

1839   Feb: Leaves Majorca for three months in Marseilles. Then to Nohant.
Publishes *L'Uscoque, Spiridion* and revised *Lélia.* Oct: Occupies adjoining apartments with Chopin until spring of 1841 at 16 rue Pigalle, Paris. Summer is spent at Nohant, with Chopin as guest.

1840   Writes *Le Compagnon du Tour de France* and *Horace.* Influenced by Pierre Leroux. Publication of *Gabriel, Cosima,* a novel based on her play.

1841   Moves from rue Pigalle to 5 and 9 rue St-Lazare, Square d'Orléans, with Chopin. Publication of *Pauline.*

1842 Vols 1 and 2 of *Consuelo* published, and *Horace*. Chopin and Delacroix at Nohant. Publishes *Un Hiver à Majorque.*

1843 Volumes 3 and 4 of *Consuelo* published, along with *Fanchette* and volumes 1 and 2 of *La Comtesse de Rudolstadt,* the sequel to *Consuelo.*

1844 *Jeanne* published, first of the pastoral novels. Also the last volumes of *La Comtesse de Rudolstadt.* Established liberal newspaper *L'Eclaireur.* Writes articles on *Politics and Socialism.*

1845 Publishes *Le Meunier d'Angibault.*

1846 Publishes *La Mare au Diable,* second pastoral novel, *lsidora* and *Teverino.*

1847 Solange marries Auguste-Jean Clésinger. Estrangement from Chopin, who has sided with Solange in a family quarrel, and whose health is deteriorating. *Lucrezia Floriani, Le Péché de M. Antoine* and *Le Piccinino* published.

1848 On behalf of the Second Republic, writes government circulars, contributes to *Bulletins de la République* and publishes her newspaper *La Cause du Peuple.* Death of Solange's newborn daughter.

1849 *La Petite Fadette* published. Birth of Solange's daughter Jeanne-Gabriel.

François le Champi successfully performed as a play at the Odéon theater in Paris.

1850 Begins liaison with Alexandre Manceau, Maurice's friend. *François le Champi* published as both play and novel.

1851 Republic falls. Plays *Claudie* and *Le Mariage de Victorine* published.

1852 Uses her influence with Louis Napoleon to save her friends from political reprisal. Solange and her husband quarrel, leave Jeanne-Gabriel with Sand at Nohant.

1853 Death of Michel de Bourges. *Les Maîtres Sonneurs, La Filleule, Mont-Reveche* published.

1854 Clésingers officially separated. Volumes 1 through 4 of *Histoire de ma Vie, Adriani* and *Flaminio* published.

1855 Jan 13: Death of Jeanne-Gabriel at school. Visit to Italy with Maurice and Alexandre Manceau. Vols 5 through 20 of *Histoire de Ma Vie* published.

1856 Does French adaptation of *As You Like It.*

1857 Death of Musset. Manceau buys cottage at Gargilesse for himself and Sand. *Le Diable aux Champs* and *La Daniella* published.

1858   Holidays at Gargilesse on River Creuse, 30 miles from Nohant, with Monceau. *Les Beaux Messieurs de Bois-Doré* published and *Légendes Rustiques,* illustrated by Maurice.

1859   Publishes *Elle et Lui, L'Homme de Neige, Les Dames Vertes, Promenades Autour d'un Village, La Guerre* and *Garibaldi.*

1860   Writes *La Ville noire* and *Marquis de Villemer.*
Nov: Contracts typhus or typhoid fever.

1862   Marriage of Maurice to Caroline Calametta. *Autour de la Table, Souvenirs et Impressions Litteraires* published.

1863   Marc-Antoine Dudevant born, son of Maurice and Caroline. Manceau and Maurice quarrel. *Mademoiselle La Quintinie* and *Pourquoi les Femmes à l'Academie?* published.

1864   Death of Marc-Antoine Dudevant. Play *Le Marquis de Villemer* presented. Moves from 3 rue Racine near the Odéon to 97 rue des Feuillantines. Leaves Nohant, because of difficulties with Maurice, to stay at Palaiseau with Manceau.

1865   Aug 21: Death of Manceau from tuberculosis, at Palaiseau. *La Confession d'une Jeune Fille* and *Laura* published.

1866 Birth of Aurore Dudevant to Maurice and Caroline. Visits Flaubert at Croisset, dedicates *Le Dernier Amour* to him. *Monsieur Sylvestre* published.

1867 Return to Nohant. Publishes *Le Dernier Amour.*

1868 Birth of Gabrielle Sand Dudevant.

1870 Play *L'Autre* with Sarah Bernhardt. *Pierre Qui Roule, Le Beau Laurence* and *Malgré Tout* published.

1871 Death of Casimir Dudevant. Seige of Paris. Sand protests Paris Commune. *Césarine Dietrich and Journal d'un Voyageur pendant la Guerre* published.

1872 Turgenev visits Nohant. *Francia* and *Nanon* published.

1873 Flaubert and Turgenev at Nohant. Travels in France. *Impressions et Souvenirs* and *Contes d'une Grand-mère* published.

1874 *Ma Soeur Jeanne* published.

1875 *Flamande* and *Les Deux Frères* published.

1876 June 8: Death of George Sand. *Le Tour de Percemont* and *Marianne Chevreuse* published.

· *Introduction* ·

"Je relèverai la femme de son abjection, et dans ma personne et dans mes écrits, Dieu m'aidera."
Correspondance IV, 18-19 (to Michel de Bourges)[1]

For decades George Sand has been recognized only as a woman who dressed like a man, smoked cigars and had love affairs with Frederic Chopin and Alfred de Musset. Only fairly recently—within the last twenty years or so—has the public been made aware that she was a prolific writer and an extraordinary intellect, a political activist who played a major role in the revolution of 1848 and participated in the great philosophical and aesthetic debates of her time.

She was one of the most popular French writers of the nineteenth century, producing about eighty novels, beginning in 1832 with *Indiana,* which became an instant bestseller. Her work was read in translation throughout Europe and the Americas. She influenced Dostoievski, Walt Whitman, the Brontës and Flaubert, among others. Like Balzac, she had to depend on her pen for her living and she met constant deadlines. By the 1850s and '60s she was writing plays which were successfully performed on the Parisian stage. Despite all this, most of her work was forgotten relatively soon after her death. It was not until the centenary of her death that she was rediscovered, thanks in part to new editions of her two-volume autobiography and twenty-five–volume correspondence, and also to the new awareness of the importance of women writers that began to develop in the late 1960s.

The two novellas presented here were first published separately in the 1830s, in serial form. They were later grouped in the 1861 Michel Lévy collection entitled *Nouvelles,* along with *Lavinia, Mattea, Metella*, and *Melchior.* We have chosen to publish these two works together because both were conceived the same year—1832—and both deal with social questions, with the theater and the condition of women—a subject always at the heart of Sand's work.

• • •

The Marquise is the story of an eighteenth-century woman, modeled after George Sand's grandmother and the grandmother's friends, for whom the young Aurore had little sympathy. The tale presents a female counterpoint to eighteenth-century libertine epistolary novels in which the woman is always the object of male desire. The Marquise is the subject of her own discourse and the observer: the role of the seducer is reversed and it is Lélio who is the object of the Marquise's desire. In the pivotal scene the lovers meet, at last, in a *petite maison,* or aristocratic trysting place, in a confusion of reality and theatrical illusion. But lust, which prevailes in libertine novels, is replaced here by chaste romantic love.

It would appear that the power of the Marquise, like that of the Marquise de Merteuil in Laclos's *Dangerous Liaisons*, is limited to the world of the salons. She has little freedom in general society. When she ventures alone into the streets of Paris, she is nearly assaulted and she cohabits for sixty years with Larrieux, a lover who provides her with protection, but whom she barely tolerates.

The male characters are portrayed in an unflattering light: both the Marquise's husband and Larrieux are interested only in sexual gratification and have no notion of romantic love or respect for the Marquise's sensibilities. By contrast, the Marquise's passion for Lélio stems from the beauty of his stage voice and presence. In reality, he is aging, unattractive, and rather vulgar; she finds this reality repulsive. She has fallen in love with a poetic illusion, an actor's impersonation, and her passion remains a solitary, unconsummated experience.

The novella is written in the form of a long monologue, in which the old Marquise tells her story to a young male visitor, who plays only a negligible part. The author here is a "conteuse," or story-teller, a form which she develops in her pastoral novels. There is also an exchange of correspondence between the Marquise and Lélio, in an echo of the eighteenth-century epistolary novel.

• • •

Pauline is longer than *The Marquise* and, like the work of Stendhal and Balzac, is written in the third person and has a contemporary realistic setting, which, along with the characters, is fully described. The story is divided into chapters and has an evolving plot. The setting is bourgeois society in the 1820s; it is removed from the aristocratic world of the salons. George Sand began writing *Pauline* in 1832, but set it aside until 1839. When one compares the characters of Laurence and the Marquise, it would seem that in those seven years the author's ideas about the condition of women evolved markedly; an evolution apparent also in the two verions of *Lélia*, where the protagonist in the 1833 version is imprisoned by her gender but is "unbound" in the 1839 revision, as Isabelle Naginski has pointed out.[2]

Despite the title, the novella concentrates on two women, Laurence and Pauline, who are foils for each other. They have begun as twin souls, their names intertwined on the mantelpiece of the village inn, but their paths in life have diverged. As adolescents, they were close friends, although Pauline was a pupil and Laurence a teacher's assistant in the girls' boarding school in their small provincial town. (It can be noted parenthetically that teaching was one of the rare liberal professions open to women in the France of the early nineteenth century, although assistant teachers were woefully underpaid, sometimes earning less than servants. The many girls' "pensions" had no religious affiliation, unlike the pre-Revolutionary convents, and most of these schools had an average enrollment of only a half-dozen students. George Sand sent her daughter Solange to this kind of school in the 1840s.)

The story begins with Pauline living an austere life, sacrificing her youth to the demands of her blind, ailing mother. When her mother dies, Laurence, who had become a well-known actress, invites Pauline to join her in Paris and share her sophisticated life. The psychology of these two women is thus juxtaposed: Laurence has earned her way by hard work, dedication and, of course, talent. The theatre for George Sand was a privileged artistic space where women were freed from society's constraints. Laurence is an intellectual: she must learn new roles and be familar with the entire classical theatrical repertoire. She reads Shakespeare to her younger sisters in the evening, hosts a salon, is financially independent, supporting her family herself and refusing to depend on any man emotionally or in any other way.

Pauline, on the other hand, has been cast by society into a saintly role which flatters her ego, but the emotional undertone of her life is one of frustration and anger. Laurence's visit at the beginning of the story is a catalyst for Pauline's restlessness. In a telling scene at the end of Part II, Pauline attempts to free her pet canary, which rejects freedom for the safety and comfort of the cage. This is an impressive metaphor for women who comply with social expectations, fearing the unknown reality outside the norm. When we first meet Pauline, she sits sewing by the window, dreaming about a greater world that she cannot explore. One is reminded of *Eugénie Grandet*, written by Balzac a year later: Eugénie, unlike Pauline, never even imagines the possibility of an escape; this makes her a saint in Balzac's eyes. For George Sand, embroidery is the symbol of women's servitude.

In 1839, she wrote *Gabriel*, a play set in sixteenth-century Italy, in which the protagonist is raised as a boy so that she can inherit her grandfather's estate. She excels at swordsmanship, mathematics, political studies, etc., and later rejects the fussy garments imposed upon her when she resumes her female role. George Sand attempted for thirty years to have this play produced in Paris, without success. It was too controversial and was not performed in the city until October, 1995.

The real heroine of this novella, then, must be Laurence, who is presented positively, while Pauline is a flawed character. Why then did George Sand call this work *Pauline*? Perhaps we can assume that Laurence is inscribed within Pauline, so to speak: Laurence is Pauline's potential.

By juxtaposing these two women, George Sand tells us that it is up to women themselves to decide what role they wish to play in society: whether they wish to move from the safe obscurity of the home to the grand stage of the world.

• • •

We have based our translation on the 1861 Michel Lévy first edition, and attempted to retain the flavor of the texts, while making them readable for a modern American audience. We have kept the original punctuation as much as possible, although occasionally semicolons have been replaced by periods or commas. Occasionally we have had to shorten elaborate sentences. This translation is the result of a rich, sustained collaboration, and we hope the reader will enjoy the fruits of our labor.

Our sincere thanks to those who have read the manuscript in search of unsightly errors and awkward phrasings: Allen Flint, Jason Wilkins, and especially Daniel Gunn and Louis Witkin. We would also like to thank those who have attended our public readings and responded with such enthusiasm to this project, Eric Paquin for his constant support, and finally our editors at Academy Chicago Publishers, without whom these novellas might still remain unaccessible to the English reading public.

SYLVIE CHARRON AND SUE HUSEMAN

Notes

[1] "I will raise women from their inferior position, in my life and through my writing, with the help of God."

[2] Isabelle Naginski: "Les deux Lélias: une réécriture exemplaire," *Revue des Sciences Humaines* 226 (1992).

✦ Preface to the First Edition ✦
(1861)

This is the first time that these novellas, written at different times and in different places, have appeared in a single volume. If some of them are fantasies of the moment, others, like *Metella* and *Pauline,* are more thoughtful stories and hence, in both form and content, more likely to survive changes in fashion. In this regard, the author would like not to defend himself,[1] but rather to explain himself to those who still occasionally reproach him for systematically placing women at the center of his compositions and for according them the best roles. Perhaps at this point he has the right to judge this sort of remark a bit outmoded, since he has achieved better gender balance in several of his novels. If some still find this insufficient, he will simply reply, "Give me time." But this reply in itself requires a brief explanation.

• • •

The author of these novellas has never had a system as to the priority of one sex over the other. He has always believed in the perfect natural equality between the sexes which is in no way altered by the diversity of their functions, since each sex finds its superiority in exercising the function that nature and Providence have accorded it. But, without returning to philosophical principles too fundamental to be debated, the author of *Pauline, Metella,* and many other similar works of fiction, would like to draw the attention of the critic and the reader to one circumstance that must be taken into account.

It is very difficult for a woman to fully understand, define, and depict an exemplary man and, especially, to *use* him as the main character in a novel. In order for a woman writer to truly understand the origin and interplay of moral forces in a man, he* must, through time, observation, and study (unjustly considered useless for someone of her sex and circumstance), become, not the man himself, which would be impossible, but a little less childlike his original education left him. He will thus come to understand the importance of certain intellectual preoccupations which were foreign to him and he will no longer restrict the masculine role to love and family relationships. If this woman writer prefers to study the passions, which are the principal focus of modern fiction, he will at least be able to show how a

---

* George Sand consistently uses the masculine pronoun to refer to the *female* author here. She plays with gender throughout the preface.

kind and learned man might use wisdom, courage, and reason to overcome adversity and his own or others' shortcomings of soul and spirit.

• • •

How much easier the task becomes when this same writer reserves all the colors of his palette to depict the female sex! He knows his own gender inside out. To be fair, we must point out that male authors also experience a great deal of difficulty when they attempt to penetrate, delicately and impartially, the mind and heart of a woman. They tend to make her too ugly or too beautiful, too weak or too strong, and those who have overcome the difficulties of this task know that it is no mean feat. We should note as well that, because his education is more complete and his power of reasoning more frequently exercised, a man can more easily depict a woman than a woman can depict a man.

Most of the novellas you are about to read belong to the author's youth: and one should always judge youth leniently. Certainly it would be unfair to pass dogmatic judgment upon what is spontaneous and consequently naïve.

GEORGE SAND
NOHANT
JANUARY, 1861

◆ | *The Marquise* | ◆

❖ *I* ❖

The Marquise of R— was not a witty woman, despite the literary notion that old ladies should sparkle with wit. She knew only what society had taught her. She did not possess the delicacy of expression, fine intelligence, or marvelous tact that is said to distinguish women of great experience. In fact, she was forgetful, abrupt, candid, even cynical on occasion. She completely shattered my notion of what an old-fashioned marquise should be like. Still, she was a Marquise, and she had seen the court of Louis XV. Since she was such an original character for her time, please do not mistake her story for a serious study of the customs of the period. Society seems so hard to understand and portray at any time that I would never presume to take on such a task. I shall limit myself to those facts that reveal the sympathetic connections between people of all societies and all times.

I had never much enjoyed the company of the Marquise. Her only remarkable quality was her extraordinary memory and the clarity with which she recounted stories from her youth. Aside from that, she was, like many old people, forgetful of the present and unconcerned about anything that did not affect her directly.

She had not been one of those unconventional beauties who must rely on wit to make an impression. Such women use their charm to compete with those more beautiful. On the contrary, the Marquise had had the misfortune of being unquestionably beautiful. I once saw the portrait that she, like so many elderly women, displayed coquettishly in her bedroom for all to admire. She was pictured as a hunting nymph and wore a satin bodice of tiger-skin design with lace sleeves, a pearl tiara in her crimped hair, and she held a sandalwood bow. In spite of all that, it was an admirable portrait of an especially admirable woman: tall, slender, dark-haired and dark-eyed, with stern yet noble features, an unsmiling ruby mouth, and hands that had been the envy of the Princess of Lamballe. Without the lace, the satin and the powder, she could have been one of those proud, agile nymphs that mortals glimpse deep in the forest or on mountainsides, only to be driven mad with love and regret.

However, the Marquise had known few amorous adventures. By her own account, she had been judged too dull. The jaded gentlemen of her time were less impressed by beauty than by alluring coquettishness. Less attractive women had stolen away her admirers, and, strangely enough, she did not seem to care. From the little she revealed about her life, it seemed to me that her heart had never been young and that self-interest had been her dominant impulse. Although I could see that genuine friendships surrounded her in old age— her grandchildren cherished her, and she was charitable without show—nevertheless, since she held to no particular principles and admitted to having no real feelings for her lover, the Viscount of Larrieux, I found no other explanation for her character than self-interest.

One evening, although she seemed depressed, she was more talkative than usual.

"My dear child," she said, "the Viscount of Larrieux has just died of the gout. It's a great sorrow to me, his friend of sixty years. And, what's more, it is terrifying to see how people die! But I'm not surprised: he was so old!"

"How old was he?" I asked.

"Eighty-four. I'm only eighty and not sickly as he was; I should hope to live longer than he did! But many of my friends have passed away this year, and even though I tell myself that I'm younger and stronger, it still frightens me to see them go."

"So those are the only regrets you have about poor Larrieux, who adored you for sixty years, forever bemoaning your rejection of him and yet never abandoning hope? He was indeed a model admirer! There are no more like him!"

"Not so," replied the Marquise with a cold smile, "the man constantly claimed to be rejected and unhappy when everyone knew that wasn't the case at all."

Seeing the Marquise in such a loquacious mood, I pressed her for more information about her relationship with the Viscount of Larrieux, and here is her odd response:

"My dear child, I know that you think I'm a very moody, irritable soul. It might be true. You be the judge. I am going to tell you my entire story and confess failings to you that I have never revealed to anyone. You, who live in a less judging time, may not find me as guilty as I find myself; but, whatever you think of me, I shall not die without having revealed myself to someone. Perhaps you'll show me enough compassion to alleviate the sadness of my memories.

"I was educated at Saint-Cyr. The brilliant education we received there really amounted to very little. I came out of school at age sixteen to marry the Marquis of R——, who was fifty. I didn't dare complain since everyone congratulated me on this wonderful marriage and all the young women without fortune envied me.

"I have never been very clever; but at that time, I was truly ignorant. My cloistered education had succeeded in numbing my already feeble faculties. I left the convent with the sort of foolish innocence some consider a virtue, but which can actually destroy one's happiness.

"Indeed, six months of marriage taught me nothing because I was too limited to appreciate it. Instead of learning about life, I started doubting myself. I came into society with some erroneous ideas and prejudices that I have never been able to overcome.

"I was not yet seventeen when I became a widow, and my mother-in-law, who had befriended me because I had such a passive nature, encouraged me to remarry. As it happened, I was also pregnant, and my modest dowry would have to be returned to my husband's family if I married again. As soon as the period of mourning had ended, I was thrust into society and surrounded by suitors. I was at the height of my beauty, and even other women admitted there was no face or figure comparable to mine.

"But my husband, a jaded old libertine who had never felt more than ironic disdain for me, and who had married me in order to secure a position, had left me with such a loathing for marriage that I would never have consented to another one. Because of my ignorance, I thought that all men were the same, that they were all hard-hearted, mercilessly ironic, and their calculating caresses humiliated and insulted me. As inexperienced as I was, I understood perfectly that my husband's rare passionate gestures were merely physical because of my beauty and that it was never a matter of the soul. Afterwards, I once again became the fool who embarrassed him in public and whom he wished he could avoid.

"This fatal first step in life disenchanted me forever. My heart, which perhaps was not destined to be

so cold, hardened with distrust. Men repelled and disgusted me. I was insulted by their attentions: I saw them
as scoundrels who acted like slaves in order to become
tyrants. I vowed eternal resentment and hatred towards
them.

"When there's no need for virtue, there is none;
that's why, even with the most austere conduct, I was
not virtuous. Oh, how I regretted it! How I envied that
moral and religious strength that combats passion and
lends color to life! My life was so cold and so empty!
What I would have given to have passions which I could
repress—and struggle to sustain—to be able to fall on
my knees and pray like the young women I saw who,
upon leaving the convent, managed to remain virtuous
for years in the midst of society because of their deter-
mination and inner strength! As for me, wretched soul,
what was I to do on this earth? Nothing but dress myself in finery, go out in public and feel bored. I had no
heart, no remorse, no fear; my guardian angel slept instead of watching over me. I found neither consolation
nor poetry in the Virgin Mary and her chaste myster-
ies. I had no need of celestial protection: I wasn't destined for danger and I was scornful of what should have
made me proud.

"For you need to understand that I blamed myself
as much as I blamed others when I discovered that my
refusal to love had degenerated into impotence. I had
often admitted, to the women who urged me to choose
a husband or lover, my aversion to the ingratitude, self-

ishness and brutality of men. Women made fun of me when I talked this way, assuring me that not all men were like my former husband, and that men had secret ways of making you forgive their vices and shortcomings. This kind of reasoning revolted me; I felt humiliated to be a woman when I heard other women express such crude sentiments and then laugh madly when I showed my indignation. For a moment, I imagined that I was worth more than all of them.

"And then I was plunged back into my grief; I was consumed by weariness. Others' lives were full, mine was empty and idle. So, I accused myself of folly and unbounded ambition; I started believing everything those worldly and cynical women had told me. They accepted their lot so easily. I thought that innocence had destroyed me, that I had impossible desires, that I had dreamed of faithful and perfect men who were not of this world. In a word, I blamed myself for all the wrongs that I had suffered.

"As long as other women thought I might soon be converted to their way of thinking—what they called their wisdom—they tolerated me. Several had great hopes that I would justify their own conduct, moving from exaggerated claims of fierce virtue to behaving loosely; they hoped I would be seen as frivolous in order to justify their own behavior.

"But when they saw that this was not working, that I was already twenty and still incorruptible, they began to detest me: they claimed that I was their critic incarnate; they ridiculed me with their lovers, and my conquest became the object of the most outrageous schemes and the most immoral enterprises. Ladies of high society were not loathe to amuse themselves by concocting infamous plots against me, and, within socially acceptable bounds, I was attacked in every way and with a relentlessness akin to hatred. There were men who promised their mistresses that they would tame me, and women who let them try. There were hostesses who offered to stupefy me with wines at dinner parties. I had friends and relatives who tempted me with men who would have made handsome coachmen for my carriage. Since I had been naïve enough to bare my soul to them, they knew full well that I held back not out of piety, or honor, or a past love, but rather out of a feeling of distrust and involuntary revulsion. They did not hesitate to reveal my character, and, without considering the confusion or the anguish of my soul, they blatantly asserted that I despised all men. There is nothing that wounds men more than this judgement; they would more easily forgive licentiousness or rebuke. Thus they shared the ladies' aversion for me; now, they courted me only to seek revenge and then laugh at me. I found irony and lies written on every face, and my misanthropy grew daily.

"A woman of character would have accepted this fate; she would have continued to resist, if only to further enrage her rivals; she would have openly claimed piety in order to attach herself to the small group of virtuous women who, even then, were respected by honest folk. But I did not have enough strength of character to face the storm that was gathering against me. I saw myself abandoned, misunderstood, hated; my reputation had already been sacrificed to the most strange and horrible accusations. Some women, themselves given to the most intense debauchery, acted as if my company threatened to corrupt them."

◆ *II* ◆

"**M**eanwhile, a man without talent, wit, energy or seductive powers arrived from the provinces. But he had a candor and honesty rare among my acquaintances. I was beginning to believe that I had to choose *someone,* as my friends suggested. Being a mother, I did not feel I had the right to remarry, because I could not rely on any man's good will. To fit into the society in which I found myself, I needed a lover. To this end, I chose this newcomer from the provinces, whose name and social status would provide sufficient protection: he was the Viscount of Larrieux.

• • •

"He loved me, with all the sincerity of his soul! But, did he have a soul? He was one of those cold, pedestrian men who lack even the elegance of vices and the cunning of lies. He loved me, rather, as my husband had sometimes loved me, in the basest manner. He was moved only by my beauty, and had no interest in my feelings. I did not find him scornful, but simply inept. If I had been able to fall in love, he would have been incapable of responding to my emotions.

"I do not think there was ever a more physical man than poor Larrieux. He ate voluptuously, fell asleep in any chair, and, the rest of the time, snuffed tobacco. Thus, he was always busy fulfilling some material need. I do not think he had as much as a single idea in a day.

"Before I became intimate with him, I considered him a friend, because even though I could not find anything redeeming about him, at least he did not seem evil. That alone made him superior to everyone else around me. I convinced myself, as I listened to his compliments, that he would reconcile me with human nature, and I trusted his loyalty. When at last I granted him those favors a woman can never reclaim, he persecuted me mercilessly with his obsessive desires, which was the only way he could express his affection.

"You can see, my friend, that I went from Charybdis to Scylla. This man, who had appeared so calm and interested only in eating and napping, could not even provide me with the friendship that I longed for. He claimed laughingly that he could not possibly remain a friend to a beautiful woman. And if you only knew what he called love! . . .

"I do not pretend to have been made from a different clay from other human beings. Now that age has made me sexless, I believe that I was as womanly as anyone else, but to develop my emotional faculties, I would have needed to have a man add a little poetry to animal instinct. Since that was not the case, you who are a man and therefore have less delicate feelings about these matters, must understand the revulsion a heart feels when it must yield to the demands of love without desire. . . . After three days, I found the Viscount of Larrieux insufferable.

"Nevertheless, the fact is, my dear, that I never had the energy to get rid of him! For sixty years, he tormented and devoured me. Civility, weakness or boredom made me tolerate him. Always unhappy at my rebuffs and yet attracted to me by the obstacles I put in the way of his passion, he pursued me with the most patient, brave, faithful and tiresome love that a man has ever bestowed on a woman.

"It was true that, since I had found a protector, my life in society had become considerably less unpleasant. Men did not dare court me; for the Viscount was a ferocious swordsman and horribly jealous. Women who had predicted that I was incapable of keeping a man were chagrined to see me in the Viscount's company; and perhaps my patience with him came partly from that vanity which forbids a woman to appear abandoned. Poor Larrieux was not much of a conquest, but he was exceedingly handsome. He was brave, knew when to keep quiet, lived stylishly, and exhibited that modest ineffectiveness that brings forth the best in a woman. Finally, while women were certainly not immune to his dull good looks, which were his worst defect in my mind, they were surprised by the sincere devotion that he showed me, and held him up as a model to their own lovers. Hence my situation became enviable, but I assure you that it was meager compensation for the nuisance of intimacy. However, I resigned myself to it and remained utterly faithful to him. I will let you judge, my child, whether I was as guilty towards him as you thought."

"I understand you perfectly," I answered. "That is why I pity and respect you. You made a dreadful sacrifice to the mores of your time, and were persecuted because you were better than those customs. Had you possessed a little more strength of character, virtue would have given you all the happiness you could not find in an amorous adventure. But let me ask one question: how could you, in the course of a lifetime, fail to meet a single man capable of understanding and converting you to true love? Should I conclude that modern men are superior to men of the past?"

"That would be very conceited on your part," she answered with a laugh. "I have very little praise for the men of my time, and yet I doubt that you have improved much; but let us not moralize. Let men be what they will; I was entirely responsible for my misfortune. I did not have enough intelligence to understand my situation. Only a superior woman with my fierce pride could have chosen, in a bird's eye view, among all those terribly dull, dishonest and empty men, a true and noble being, a rare exception in any period. I was too ignorant, too limited for that. After a while, I became a better judge. I realized that some men, all of whom I had lumped together in my hatred, deserved better; but by then I was old and it was too late."

"And, while you were still young," I insisted, "were you not tempted even once to try again: was this passionate aversion never shaken? That is strange!"

· III ·

The Marquise fell silent for a moment; then, abruptly, letting the gold snuff box she had been fingering fall onto the table, she said:

"Well, since I have begun my confession, I might as well tell you everything. Listen carefully:

"Once, just once in my life, I fell in love, in love as no one has ever been. It was a passionate, uncontrollable, all-devouring, yet ideal and platonic love. Oh! You seem astonished to learn that a marquise of the eighteenth century had only one great love in her lifetime and a platonic love at that! You see, my child, you young men think that you understand women, but you know nothing about them. If eighty-year-old women started giving truthful accounts of their lives, you might well discover vices and virtues of the feminine character that you never imagined. Now can you imagine the social origins of the man for whom I completely lost my head, I, a marquise, the haughtiest and proudest of marquises?"

"The King of France or the Dauphin, Louis XVI."

"Oh! If you start there, it will take you hours to get to the object of my affections. I would rather tell you: he was an actor."

"Then he was still a king, I imagine."

"The noblest and most elegant ever to appear on stage. You are not surprised?"

"Not really. I have heard that such uneven matches were not rare even when class prejudices were stronger in France. Which of the friends of Madame d'Epinay was it who lived with Jeliotte?"

"How well you know our times! How sad! The very fact that such cases are recorded in diaries and noted with astonishment should help you understand how rare they were and how contrary to the customs of the time. You can be sure that they created quite a scandal back then. When you are told of the horrible depravity of the Duke of Guiche and of Manicamp, of Madame Lionne and her daughter, you can rest assured that they shocked people as much then as now. Do you really believe that those whose indignant pens recorded these affairs were the only scrupulous souls in France?"

I did not dare contradict the Marquise. And I did not know which one of us was better equipped to decide the question. With my encouragement, she continued her story:

"Just to prove to you how little tolerance there was, let me tell you that when I first saw him and expressed my admiration to the Countess of Ferrières who was sitting next to me, she replied: 'You should think twice, my lovely, before praising him so warmly to someone besides me. Others would mock you cruelly if they thought you had forgotten that in the eyes of a well-born woman, an actor cannot be considered a man.'

"Madame De Ferrière's words stuck in my mind, I don't know why. At that time, her scorn seemed absurd to me; and her fear that I might compromise myself through my admiration appeared hypocritical and mean-spirited.

"His name was Lélio. He was Italian by birth, but he spoke French beautifully. He may have been thirty-five, although on stage he often seemed less than twenty. He played Corneille better than Racine, but he did both exceptionally well."

"I am surprised," I said, interrupting the Marquise, "that his name is not included among the great names of the theatre."

"He never had much of a reputation," she replied. "He was not esteemed either in town or at court. I heard that at his theatrical debut he was booed mercilessly. Later, he was recognized for the emotional depth of his portrayals and for his efforts to improve his craft. He was tolerated and sometimes applauded, but on the whole he was considered an actor of mediocre talent.

"He was a man who was no more at home with the theatrical conventions of his time than I was with the social conventions of my world. Perhaps that is the intangible, all-powerful affinity that drew our souls together from opposite ends of the social spectrum. The public had understood Lélio no better than society had judged me.

"'This man is overly dramatic,' they said of him, 'he exaggerates and feels nothing.'

"And of me they said: 'That woman is haughty and cold; she has no heart.'

"Who knows, perhaps the two of us felt more deeply than any of them.

"In those days, tragedies were played with *decorum*. Even a slap was done in good taste. One died properly and collapsed with grace. Dramatic art was fashioned after the conventions of high society. The actors' speech and gestures matched the hoop skirts and powdered wigs that even Phèdre and Clytemnestra had to wear. I had not sensed or recognized the flaws in this theatrical style. I had not reflected much; I simply knew that tragedy bored me to tears. Since it would have been bad form to admit it, I courageously went off to be bored twice a week. Nevertheless, because of the cold, restrained manner with which I listened to those pompous tirades, I was said to be insensitive to the charm of beautiful verse.

"I had been absent from Paris a rather long time when I returned one evening to the Comédie Française to see *The Cid*.[1] During my stay in the country Lélio had been permitted to join the troupe and I was seeing him there for the first time. He was playing Rodrigue. The moment I heard the sound of his voice, I was moved. His voice was penetrating rather than sonorous, a distinct, vibrant voice—one of the things for which he was criticized. The Cid was expected to have a deep voice, just as classical heroes were supposed to be tall and strong. A king who measured less than five feet six inches simply could not wear the crown; it would be contrary to good taste.

"Lélio was short and thin; his beauty was not in his features, but in the nobility of his forehead, in the irresistible grace of his stance, in his freedom of movement, in his proud and melancholy expression. I have never seen, in a statue, a painting, or a man, a more powerful beauty, more ideal or more natural. The word 'charm' should have been invented for him, for it characterized his speech, his looks, his every movement.

"How can I explain? It was as if he cast a spell on me. This man, who walked, spoke and acted without artifice or pretension, who sobbed with his heart as much as with his voice, who forgot himself in his passion; this man whose soul seemed to consume and destroy him, whose gaze held all the love I had vainly sought in this world, exercised over me a truly electrifying power. This man, who was not born in an era where he could claim the glory and sympathy he deserved, who had only me to understand him and serve as his following, was, for five years, my king, my god, my life and my love.

"I could no longer live without seeing him: he controlled and dominated me. He was not a suitable match for me, but I disagreed with Madame de Ferrières; he was quite superior: he was a moral force, an intellectual master, whose soul molded mine at his will. Soon it became impossible to hide the effect that he had on me. I gave up my box at the Comédie Française in order not to betray myself. I pretended that I had become devout and that I was going to church every evening to pray. Instead, I dressed as a simple working girl and mixed with the common folk at the theatre in order to hear him and observe him as I pleased. Eventually I won over one of the employees at the theatre and managed to secure a narrow, secret space in a corner of the theatre that I could reach by means of a hidden passage and where no one could see me. To be even more secure, I dressed as a schoolboy.

"These follies, which I committed for a man with whom I had never exchanged a word or a look, offered me the thrill of mystery and the illusion of happiness. When the hour for the theatre chimed on the enormous clock in my living room, I was seized with violent palpitations. I tried to compose myself while my servants prepared my carriage. I paced in agitation and if Larrieux was with me I bullied him to make him leave. I artfully avoided all other unwanted callers as well. The cunning that my passion for theatre gave me was amazing. I had to have a great deal of guile and cleverness indeed to successfully hide my feelings from Larrieux, the most jealous of men, and from all the wicked people who surrounded me, and to do so for five years.

"I must admit that rather than struggle against my passion, I gave myself over to it eagerly, cheerfully. It was so pure! Why should I have felt ashamed? It gave me new life; it initiated me at last into everything I had longed to know and to feel. And, to a certain degree, it made me a woman.

"I was happy. I was proud to feel myself tremble, struggle for breath, and grow faint. The first time a violent throb awoke my sleeping heart, I was as proud as a young expectant mother who feels the first movement of the child in her womb. I became sulky, mocking, mischievous, moody. Poor Larrieux commented that my passion had made me strangely capricious. In social circles I was said to grow more beautiful every day; my black eyes became velvety, my smile thoughtful, and my remarks about everything displayed more depth and insight than anyone had thought me capable of. Everyone gave Larrieux credit although he, of course, had nothing to do with it.

"My memories of this part of my life are somewhat disjointed because they engulf me so completely. As I share them with you, it seems to me that I am young again and that my heart still pounds at the name of Lélio. A little while ago I was telling you how I used to tremble with joy and impatience when the clock chimed. Even now it seems to me that I can still feel the delicious breathlessness that used to seize me at the sound of that chime. Since that time, the vicissitudes of fortune have been such that I feel quite happy to find myself in a tiny apartment in the Marais district. I do not miss anything about my luxurious home, my fine neighborhood, my past splendor, except those few objects which would have reminded me of my lost love and dreams. I managed to save from the disaster of emigration some of my old furnishings, and they evoke the same feelings as if the hour were chiming and my horses' hooves were pawing the cobblestones. Oh, my child, do not ever love that way, for it unleashes a storm that only death can quell!

"And so I set off, alive, carefree, young and happy! I was beginning to appreciate all that my life contained: the luxury, the youth, the beauty. Happiness pervaded every sense, every pore of my being. Softly nestled in the depths of my carriage, my feet enveloped in furs, I contemplated my reflection, radiant and adorned, in the gold-framed mirror facing me. Feminine fashion at that time, which has been greatly ridiculed since, was of extraordinary brilliance and splendor. When worn with taste and purity in its exaggeration, it lent a nobility and flowing grace to feminine beauty that paintings fail to capture. Thus bedecked in feathers and fabric, a woman was obliged to move with a certain slow majesty. I have seen very pale ladies who, powdered and dressed in white, trailing their long silky trains and gracefully balancing their head plumes, could, without exaggeration, be compared to swans. Despite what Rousseau wrote on the subject, it was birds rather than wasps that we resembled with our enormous folds of satin, with that profusion of chiffon puffs that hid a frail little body the way down hides a turtledove, with the long lace wings that drooped from our arms, with our skirts of bright, variegated colors, our ribbons and our jewels. And when we carefully balanced ourselves on tiny feet in heeled slippers, as though we were afraid to touch the ground, we walked with the dainty caution of a shepherdess along the bank of a meadow brook.

"During this same period, people began to powder their hair to achieve a soft ashen tint. This practice lent a great deal of softness to the face and an extraordinary brilliance to the eye. The forehead, entirely revealed, blended into the pale shades of the powdered hair; it appeared wider and purer, and lent a noble air to every woman. The towering hairdos, which I had never found graceful, gave way to lower hair styles with plump curls drawn back, cascading over neck and shoulders. This hairstyle was extremely becoming to me and I was known for the richness and originality of my accessories. At times I wore a red velvet dress decorated with grebe feathers, at others a tunic of white satin trimmed with tiger skin, occasionally an outfit of lilac damask threaded with silver and white plumes mounted in pearls. Thus adorned, I made a few visits while waiting for the second play to begin; for Lélio never acted in the first.

"I caused a sensation in the salons and when I climbed back into my carriage. I saw with satisfaction the woman who loved Lélio and who could surely make him love her. Until then, the only pleasure I had found in being beautiful was the jealousy I inspired. The care I took in enhancing this beauty was benign vengeance against the women who had concocted such horrible plots against me. But, from the moment I fell in love, I began to take personal pleasure in my own beauty. That is all I had to offer Lélio to compensate for the triumphs Paris denied him, and I amused myself by imagining the proud pleasure of this poor actor who had been so mocked, so misunderstood, so rebuffed, the day he learned that the Marquise of R— worshiped him.

• • •

"However, these were just pleasant, fleeting dreams; the only result and only profit I drew from my situation. As soon as my thoughts materialized and I perceived the slightest firmness in whatever plan my love had formed, I courageously abandoned it, and all the pride of rank reasserted its dominion over my soul. You are looking at me with surprise? I will explain all that to you later. For the moment, let me dwell in the enchanted world of memory.

"Towards eight o'clock I had myself transported to the little Church of the Carmelites near the Luxembourg palace; I sent the carriage away on the pretext that I was attending a lecture on religion to be held at that hour; but I simply cut through the church and the courtyard, and came out into another street. I went to the garret of a young working-class woman named Florence who was completely devoted to me. I shut myself in her room and gleefully threw my clothing on her bed in order to don the square black tunic, the sword in shagreen sheath and the symmetrical wig of a young schoolmaster studying for the priesthood. Given my height, complexion, and inoffensive look, I had just the awkward, hypocritical air of a young priest disguising himself to go off to the theatre. Florence, who imagined some genuine intrigue on my part, laughed with me at my metamorphosis, and I admit that I could not have been happier if I had been preparing for an evening of intoxicating pleasure and passion like all those foolish young women who attended clandestine suppers in *petite maisons*, secret hideaways.[2]

"I climbed into another carriage, and went off to huddle in my tiny theatre box. Once there, my trembling, my terror, my joy, and my impatience ceased! I fell into a deep trance and remained that way, absorbed until the curtain rose, awaiting a grand and solemn event.

"Just as a vulture envelops a partridge in his magnetic flight, holds her panting and motionless in the magical circle that he draws above her, the soul of Lélio, the grand soul of a tragic hero and poet, enveloped all my senses and held me enthralled. I listened to him with my hands clasped around my knees, my chin resting on the velvet cover of the stage box, my forehead bathed in sweat. I held my breath, cursed the glare of the chandeliers straining my eyes as I followed his every gesture, his every step. I wanted to feel every tremor of his bosom, to see every furrow in his brow. His feigned emotions, his theatrical misfortunes, moved me as though they were real. I could no longer distinguish between fantasy and reality. Lélio no longer existed. He was Rodrigue, Bajazet, Hippolyte.[3] I hated his enemies, I feared the dangers he faced; I shed torrents of tears for his sufferings; his death tore from me screams that I smothered by biting my handkerchief. During intermissions, I would collapse exhausted in the back of my box. I would stay there corpse-like until the shrill sound of the bell announced the curtain's rise. Then I would come back to life, once again mad with passion, ready to admire, to be moved and to weep. What youth, poetry and vigor there was in this man's talent! The entire generation must have been made of ice not to fall at his feet.

"And yet, even though he did not fit the common mold, could not please the foolish tastes of the public, scandalized the ladies with his unkempt appearance, the gentlemen with his scorn for their ridiculous protocols, he had moments of sublime power and irresistible attraction during which he held this unwilling, unappreciative audience in the palm of his hand, forcing it to tremble and applaud. Because the values of a century change slowly, these moments were rare; but when it happened, he received frenetic applause. It seemed that Parisians, momentarily awed by his genius, tried to atone for their slights. I felt that this man occasionally possessed a supernatural power, and that his most bitter critics were compelled to let him triumph in spite of themselves. Indeed, on these occasions, the public at the Comédie Française seemed bewitched and, as they left, people were amazed that they had applauded Lélio. As for me, I would take these opportunities to indulge my emotions; I would scream, cry, call out his name, beckon him passionately. Fortunately, my voice was lost in the storm that exploded around me.

"At other times, he was booed in scenes where I found him sublime, and I would leave the performance in a rage. Those days were the most dangerous for me. I was greatly tempted to seek him out, to weep with him, to curse our century and to console him by offering him my admiration and my love.

"One night as I was leaving through the hidden passage that I used, I saw in front of me a short, slender man moving toward the street. A stagehand tipped his hat to him, saying: 'Good night, Monsieur Lélio.'

"Eager to take a closer look at this extraordinary man, I hurried after him, crossed the street, and without a thought for the danger I might face, followed him into a small café. Luckily it was a disreputable place where I did not risk meeting anyone of my circle.

"When, under the dim light of a smoky chandelier, I looked at Lélio, I thought I had followed the wrong man. He was at least thirty-five years old, had a sallow, yellowish complexion and looked worn-out. He was poorly dressed and common-looking, and he spoke with a hoarse, flat voice; he seemed at home with ruffians, guzzling brandy and swearing at leisure. I had to hear his name called several times to believe that there stood the theatrical idol, the interpreter of the great Corneille. I no longer saw any of the charm which had fascinated me, not even his noble, sad and ardent gaze. His look was gloomy, lifeless, almost stupid; his careful enunciation turned vile as he addressed a waiter and spoke of gambling, cabarets and women. His walk was a slouch, his clothing was stained and dirty, and his cheeks were soiled with makeup. He was no longer Hippolyte, he had become Lélio. The temple was empty and desolate, the oracle was mute, God had become a man; not even a man—an actor.

"He left, and I stayed in my seat for a long time, astounded, forgetting to drink the hot spicy wine I had ordered with bravado. When I eventually realized where I was and the looks I was getting, I was seized with fright. Never before in my life had I found myself in so compromising a situation, in direct contact with this class of people; since then, emigration has inured me to awkward circumstances like that one.

"I got up and started to leave, but I hadn't paid. The waiter ran after me. I was mortified; I had to return, explain myself at the counter, endure all those accusatory mocking stares. Once outside, I felt that I was being followed. I searched in vain for a cab to take me away; there were none left in front of the Comédie. I could hear heavy steps behind me. Trembling, I turned and saw a great lout whom I had noticed in a corner of the café; he looked like a spy or something worse. He spoke to me; I do not know what he said, I was paralyzed with fear and yet I had the presence of mind to escape him. With a courage born from fear, I became a true heroine; I struck him in the face with my cane and, throwing it aside while he stood stunned at my audacity, I took off like a shot and did not stop running until I reached Florence's garret. When I awoke the next day in my own bed with its padded curtains and pink-feathered cornices, I thought at first that I had dreamed it all, and then felt greatly embarassed by my disillusionment and the previous day's escapade. I seriously believed that I was cured of my infatuation and tried to take pride in it, but could not. I felt a mortal regret; boredom once again pervaded my life; the spell was broken. I threw Larrieux out that very day.

"Evening came but no longer brought the welcome turbulence of other evenings. Salon society seemed insipid to me. I went to church and listened to the sermon, determined to become devout; I caught a cold and went home feeling ill.

"I stayed in bed for several days. The Countess of Ferrières visited me and assured me that I had no fever, that staying in bed made me worse, that I must look for distractions, get out, go to the Comédie. I think that she had designs on Larrieux and wanted me dead.

"Things turned out differently; she forced me to accompany her to the performance of *Cinna*.

"'You don't come to the theatre anymore,' she said. 'Religion and boredom are wearing you out. It's been a long time since you have seen Lélio; he has improved, he sometimes gets applause now; I have a hunch that he will become bearable.'

"I don't know why I let her tempt me. But, disenchanted as I was with Lélio, at least I no longer risked losing control when confronted with his seductiveness in public. I dressed lavishly and entered our stage-box to brave a danger which I no longer believed existed.

"But danger had never been closer. Lélio was sublime and I realized that I had never been more in love. My previous misadventure seemed only a dream; it was impossible to believe that Lélio could be different from the way he appeared on stage. In spite of myself, I succumbed once more to the violent emotions that he alone evoked in me. I had to hide my tearful face in my handkerchief; in my confusion, I smeared my rouge and lost my beauty marks, and the Countess of Ferrières urged me to withdraw to the rear of the stage-box, because my conduct was creating quite a stir in the audience. Luckily, I had the presence of mind to pretend that my emotional state was in response to the performance of Mademoiselle Hippolyte Clairon.[4] In reality, I found her a very cold, unemotional actress, perhaps too haughty by education and temperament for the theatrical profession as it was practiced then; but the way she pronounced 'so beautiful' in *Cinna* had given her a fine reputation.

"Nevertheless, it is true that when she acted with Lélio, her performance improved immeasurably. Although she displayed a fashionable scorn for his method, she was influenced by his genius without realizing it; she seemed inspired by him when they played love scenes.

"That evening, Lélio noticed me, either because of my attire or my emotion, for as he went offstage, I saw him turn to one of the gentlemen whose rank permitted him to sit on stage, and ask for my name. I gathered that from the way they were looking at me. My heart was beating so hard that I almost fainted, and I noticed that during the rest of the play, Lélio looked in my direction more than once. I would have given the world to find out what the Chevalier de Brétillac had said about me; Lélio had questioned him and he had replied several times while staring at me! Lélio had to keep a serious face not to detract from the dignity of his role, and he did not show any signs that would allow me to guess what kind of information he had received about me. Moreover, I hardly knew this Brétillac; I could not imagine what he could have to say of me, good or ill.

"It was precisely that night that I first understood the nature of the love which bound me to Lélio: it was a purely intellectual and romantic passion. It was not him I loved, but the classic hero that he represented;

those feelings of honesty, loyalty and tenderness, for-ever lost, which lived once again in him. I found my-self transported with him and through him to a period of now-forgotten virtues. I was proud enough to be-lieve that in earlier times I would not have been mis-understood and slandered, that I could have given my heart and not been reduced to loving a theatrical ghost. Lélio was a mere shadow of the Cid, a symbol of an-cient and chivalrous love now ridiculed in France. The man himself, the stage actor, did not affect me in the least. I had seen him; I could love him only on stage. My own Lélio was a fictitious being who no longer existed for me once the theatre lights went out. Only the illusion of the stage, the reflection of the chande-liers, the makeup and costumes could conjure up the man I loved. Stripped of all that, he disappeared; like a star, he faded with the light of dawn. Offstage I no longer had the slightest desire to see him, and would in fact have been devastated if I *had* seen him. It would have been like seeing a great man reduced to a few ashes in a clay urn.

"My frequent absences at times when I had usu-ally received Larrieux, and, in particular, my refusal to continue to be anything more than a friend to him, in-spired a fit of jealousy more justified, I confess, than any he had experienced previously. One night, on my way to the Carmelite convent where I intended to slip out the side door, I noticed that he was following me and realized that it was going to be nearly impossible to conceal my nocturnal escapades from him. So I decided to go openly to the theatre. Gradually, I gained control enough to hide my feelings, and I began to profess immense admiration for Hippolyte Clairon in order to mask my true feelings. I was now more restricted; because I was forced to monitor my behavior, my pleasure was less keen and less deeply felt. But this situation quickly gave birth to another compensation. Lélio now could see me; he could observe me. He had been struck by my beauty, flattered by my responsiveness. He could hardly keep his eyes off me. At times, he was so distracted that the audience was annoyed. I could no longer be mistaken: he was madly in love with me.

"The Princess of Vaudemont envied my theatre box so I gave it to her in exchange for a smaller one, less conspicuous and better situated. I was right above the edge of the stage; I caught Lélio's every glance and his eyes sought mine without risk of compromise. Furthermore, I no longer needed to see him to share his every emotion: the sound of his voice, his heartfelt sighs, the emphasis he gave to certain lines, to certain words, told me that he was addressing me. I was the proudest and happiest of women at those moments, for I was loved not by the actor but by the hero he portrayed.

"Now, after two years of a secret solitary infatuation that I had nourished in the depths of my soul, three more winters passed with this newly shared love, without my ever casting a glance that might cause him to hope for more than this intimate yet mysterious bond.

I have learned since that Lélio often followed me when I went out; but I never bothered to notice him or to seek him out in the crowd, for I had little desire to see him outside the theatre. Those years are the only five of my eighty in which I have felt truly alive.

"Finally, one day, in the *Mercure de France*, I read the name of a new actor who had been hired by the Comédie Française to replace Lélio, who was to travel abroad. This news dealt me a mortal blow; I could not conceive of a life without this emotion, without this passionate and stormy existence. This threat increased my love immeasurably and nearly brought about my ruin.

"I no longer tried to suppress any emergent thought unworthy of the dignity of my rank. I no longer rejoiced in Lélio's shortcomings as a man. I suffered and secretly regretted that he was not what he appeared to be on stage, and I even wished that he were as young and handsome as artifice made him each night so that I could sacrifice to him all my proud prejudices and all my physical aversion. Now that I was about to lose the idealized being who had filled my soul for so long, I wanted to realize my dreams and taste material reality even if I were to hate life, Lélio and myself afterwards.

"I was still filled with indecision when I received a letter written in an unfamiliar hand; it is the only love letter that I have kept from among the thousands of protestations written by Larrieux and the thousands of perfumed declarations from a hundred others. It is in fact the only real love letter I have ever received."

The Marquise interrupted herself, got up, and, with a sure hand, opened an inlaid chest from which she drew a worn, crumpled letter which I read with difficulty.

Madame,

I feel certain that this letter can only inspire your scorn; you will find it unworthy of your anger. But for a man falling into an abyss, what difference can one more stone thrown after him make? You will think me a fool, and rightfully so. And yet you may secretly pity me, for you cannot doubt my sincerity. If religion has made you compassionate, then perhaps you will understand the extent of my despair; you must know already, Madame, the power your eyes hold to do good or evil.

And so, if I can draw one compassionate thought from you, if tonight, at the eagerly awaited hour each evening when I begin to live again, I can read in your face the slightest expression of pity, I promise it will alleviate my misery when I will carry away from France one memory that may give me the strength to live elsewhere and to pursue my difficult and thankless career.

But you must already know this; I cannot believe that my troubled state, my emotional outbursts, my cries of anger and despair have not betrayed me a dozen times on stage. You could not have inspired such flames of passion without some awareness of what you were doing. Ah! Perhaps you were playing with me like a lion with its prey, perhaps you were amusing yourself with my torment and my folly.

But, no! That is too presumptuous. No, Madame, I do not believe it; you never dreamed of doing that. You appreciate the poetry of the great Corneille, you respond to the noble passions of tragedy: that is all. And I foolishly dared to believe that my voice alone sometimes aroused your sympathy, that my heart found an echo in yours, that there was something more between the two of us than between me and the public. Oh! It was an unworthy but tender folly! Do not take it away from me, Madame; what harm can it do? Could you be afraid that I would brag about it? By what right could I and how would I prove my claim? I could only attract the ridicule of honest folk. I beg of you, let me hold on to this conviction, that I embrace with fervor; it has brought me more happiness than public disfavor has brought me pain. Let me bless you, thank you on my knees, for the sensitivity that I discovered in your soul, and that no other soul has granted me; for those tears that I saw you shed for the woes I portrayed and that carried my inspiration to new heights; for those timid glances which attempted, or so I believed, to console me for the unresponsiveness of the audience.

Oh, why were you born to such brilliance and splendor? Why am I only a poor artist without fame or glory? Why can't I have public acclaim and a banker's wealth to pay for a title, one of those aristocratic names I have always disdained but that might allow me to hope for your favors? I used to prefer the distinction of talent to any other; I wondered what good it was to be a Chevalier or a Marquis if it meant only being foolish, vain and overbearing; I hated the arrogance of the aristocrats and avenged myself by rising above them through my genius as an actor.

What impossible dreams and disappointment! My strength has failed my wild ambitions. I have remained obscure; worse yet, I have flirted with success and let it slip away. I thought I had achieved greatness and was cast aside; I imagined that I had reached the sublime and was condemned to ridicule. Destiny took my boundless dreams and my audacious soul, and broke me like a reed! What a wretched man I am!

But my greatest folly was to have cast my eyes beyond the stage rail that marked an invisible line between me and the rest of society. It was like Popilius' circle to me. Why did I wish to step beyond it! I, a mere actor, dared to have eyes and to fix them upon a beautiful woman! A woman so young, so noble, so loving and so highborn! For you are all of that, Madame, I know it well. Society accuses you of being cold and excessively pious. I alone know you and can judge you. A single smile, a single tear from you was enough to belie the stupid gossip that the Chevalier de Brétillac had spread about you.

But then what uncommon destiny is yours as well? What strange fate broods over you and me, so that in the midst of such brilliant society, one that claims to be so enlightened, you found only the heart of a poor actor to give you justice? Nothing can take away this sad but comforting thought: if we had been born into the same social sphere, you would not have been able to escape me, whoever my rivals might have been, no matter how mediocre I might have been. You would have had to recognize this truth, that I possess something greater than their fortunes and their titles: the ability to love you.

Lélio.

"This letter," the Marquise added, "strange for the time in which it was written, seemed so strong and true to me in spite of a few Racinian clichés in the beginning, and I found in it a passion so bold and new that I was deeply moved. The remnants of pride I had been struggling against vanished. I would have given my entire life for one hour of such passion.

"I will not relate my anxiety, my fantasies, my fears; I myself cannot remember why or how they came to be. I answered with the following few words, as best I can remember:

I do not blame you, Lélio, I blame fate; I pity not only you but myself as well. Not caution, pride, nor prudishness could prompt me to withdraw from you the consolation of believing that I have singled you out. Hold on to it, for it is the only consolation I can offer. I can never consent to see you.

"The next day, I received a brief note that I read hastily and threw into the fire just in time to hide it from Larrieux, who saw me reading it. It read more or less like this:

> Madame, I must speak to you or I will die. Once, only once, and only for an hour if you wish. What can you possibly fear from meeting me, since you have confidence in my honor and my discretion? Madame, I know who you are: I know what you have been, I know you are devout, and I even know your feelings for Viscount Larrieux. I am not foolish enough to hope for anything more than a word of pity; but I must receive it directly from your lips; my heart must gather it in and carry it away, or my heart will break.
>
> Lélio.

"I will say in my defense, for complete trust is noble and courageous in the face of danger, that I was never afraid for an instant of being mocked by an impudent roué. I believed faithfully in Lélio's humble sincerity. Moreover, I was rewarded for trusting in my strength; I decided to see him. I had completely forgotten his ravaged face, his bad manners, his common look; I thought only of his genius, his eloquence and his love. I replied to him:

> I will meet you. Find a safe place; but expect no more from me than you have asked. I have faith

in you as I do in God. If you were to abuse my trust, you would be a villain and I would not fear you.

"His answer:

> Your faith would save you from the worst of scoundrels. You will see, Madame, that Lélio is not unworthy of it. The Duke of —— has often been kind enough to offer me his house in Rue de Valois; what would I have done with it? For three years no other woman has existed for me under heaven. Would you be willing to meet me there after the theatre?

"He gave me directions to the house.

"I received this message at four o'clock. All these discussions had taken place in a single day. I had spent the day wandering through my apartment like a lost soul. I was feverish. The fast pace of these events and decisions, after five years of resolutions to the contrary, swept me away as in a dream; and, when I had made the final decision, when I saw that I had committed myself and that it was too late to retreat, I fell onto the sofa, breathless, as the room whirled about me.

"I was extremely ill; a surgeon had to be summoned to bleed me. I forbade my servants to say a word to anyone about my condition; I feared meddlers would offer me gratuitous advice, and I did not want anyone to prevent me from going out that night. Waiting for the appointed hour, I threw myself on my bed and barred even Larrieux from my door.

"The effects of the bleeding were soothing but enervating. I became depressed; all my illusions disappeared with the fever. I recovered my memory and my reason; I remembered my terrible disappointment at the café, Lélio's vulgar appearance; I was ready to blush at my foolishness, to plunge from the pinnacle of illusion into a flat and ignoble reality. I could no longer understand how I could have decided to barter this heroic, romantic tenderness against the disgust that awaited me and the shame that would poison all my memories. I felt a mortal regret for what I had done; I wept for the happiness, the life of love, and the future of pure, intimate pleasure that I was about to destroy. I wept most of all for Lélio; by seeing him, I was going to lose him forever. I had loved him so happily for five years, and in a few hours I would no longer be able to love him.

"In my distress, I wrung my hands violently, reopening my wound, and the blood flowed profusely; I barely had time to ring for my maid who found me unconscious on my bed. A deep, heavy sleep, that I struggled against in vain, took hold of me. I did not dream, I did not suffer, I lay as if dead for several hours. When I opened my eyes, my room was dark, my house quiet; my servant was asleep in a chair at the foot of my bed. I remained numb and weak for a while without thought or memory.

"Then, suddenly, I remember. I ask myself whether the time and the day of the rendezvous have passed, if I have slept an hour or a century, if it is day or night, if I have killed Lélio by not keeping my word, if there is still time. I try to get up, my strength fails me; I struggle for a while as in a nightmare. Finally, I summon all my willpower to lift my heavy limbs. I hurry to the window and pull aside the curtains; I see the moon shining on the trees in the garden; I run to the clock: ten o'clock. I rush to my chambermaid and shake her awake.

"'Quinette, what day is it?'

"She leaps from her chair with a cry and tries to run away, thinking me delirious; I restrain and reassure her; I learn that I have slept only three hours. I thank God. I ask for a carriage; Quinette looks at me, dumbfounded. Finally, convinced that I am rational, she conveys my request and starts to help me dress.

"I had the simplest, most demure of my dresses brought to me; I wore my hair unadorned; I refused to put on makeup. I wanted above all to inspire in Lelio the esteem and the respect that were more precious to me than his love. Nevertheless I felt pleased when Quinette, surprised at my behavior, said, surveying me from head to foot:

"'Really, Madame, I don't know how you manage; you're wearing only a simple white dress without train or hoop; you are ill and pale as death; you haven't even added a beauty mark: yet I swear that I have never seen you more beautiful than tonight. I pity the men who will see you!'

"'Then you think me very virtuous, my dear Quinette?'

"'Alas, Madame, I ask Heaven every day to help me be like you; but so far . . .'

"'Never mind, dear innocent, give me my coat and my muff.'

"At midnight I arrived at the house in the rue Valois. I was heavily veiled. Some sort of butler appeared to let me in; he was the only person visible in this mysterious dwelling. He led me through a dark garden to a small house hidden in silence and shadows. After setting his lantern of green silk in the reception hall, he opened the door of a long, dark apartment, pointed politely to the ray of light emanating from the end of the hallway and said in a low voice, as if he were afraid of awakening sleeping echoes:

"'Madame is alone; no one else has arrived yet. Madame will find a bell in the summer sitting room to summon me if she needs anything.'

"Then he disappeared as if by magic, closing the door behind him.

"I was seized by a horrible fear; I was afraid I had fallen into a trap. I called after him; he appeared immediately. His air of stolid stupidity reassured me. I asked him what time it was; I knew perfectly well since I had consulted my watch a dozen times in the carriage.

"'It is midnight,' he replied without looking at me.

"I understood that this was a man carefully trained in his duties. I decided to go into the summer salon and was convinced that my fears were groundless when I saw that all of the doors opening onto the garden were merely partitions of painted silk. Nothing could have been more delightful than this boudoir, which was actually a simple music room. The walls were made of stucco as white as snow; the frames of the mirrors were unpolished silver, musical instruments of extraordinary richness were scattered about on white velvet furniture with pearl edging. All the light in the room came from the ceiling but was hidden behind alabaster leaves arranged in a rotunda effect. One could have mistaken this cool soft illumination for moonlight. I looked with great interest at this retreat that was unlike anything I could remember seeing. It was and would be the only time in my life that I had set foot in a *petite maison*; but either because this room was not the one used for assignations, or because Lélio had had removed any object that I might find offensive, my inital repugnance quickly faded away. A single statue of white marble stood in the center; it was quite old: a veiled Isis holding one finger to her lips. The mirrors around us reflected us together, both pale, dressed in white, and chastely veiled. The illusion was so powerful that I had to move to separate her image from mine.

"Suddenly, this silence, that I found sad, frightening, and at the same time delicious, was interrupted;

the far door opened and closed: light steps creaked softly on the parquet floor. I sank into a chair more dead than alive; I was about to see Lélio close up outside the theatre. I lowered my eyes and silently bade him farewell before looking up again.

"But what a surprise! Lélio was as handsome as the angels; he had not taken the time to remove his theatrical costume: it was the most elegant I had seen him in. His slender waist was wrapped in a Spanish belt of white satin. His shoulder and garter bows were of cherry red ribbon; a short jacket of the same color was thrown over his shoulders. He wore an enormous English ruff, his hair was short and unpowdered under a jaunty cap decorated with white feathers and a glittering diamond rosette. This was the costume in which he had just played the role of Don Juan in the *Festin de Pierre*.[5] I had never seen him look so handsome, so young, so romantic as at that moment. Velasquez would have bowed in admiration.

"He knelt at my feet. I could not keep myself from giving him my hand. He had such a hesitant, submissive air! A man smitten to the point of timidity before a woman was so rare in those days! And a thirty-five-year-old man, an actor!

"Despite his age, it seemed to me, it still seems to me today, that he was in the full bloom of adolescence. In his white costume he looked like a young page; his forehead had all the purity, his pounding heart all the ardor of a first love. He took my hands and covered them with kisses. Then I went mad; I drew his head down upon my knees; I caressed his burning forehead, his rough black hair, his tanned neck lost in the whiteness of the collar . . . and Lelio did not become emboldened. All of his emotion was concentrated in his heart; he began to cry like a woman; I was flooded by his tears.

"Oh! I admit that I delighted in letting my own tears mingle with his. I forced him to raise his head and look at me. How handsome he was, dear God! What fire and tenderness were in his eyes! How the truth and generosity of his soul lent charm even to the flaws in his features ravaged by dissipation and time! Oh! The strength of the soul! Anyone who has not understood its miracles has never loved! As I saw the early wrinkles on his beautiful forehead, the wistfulness of his smile, the pallor of his lips, I was touched. I wanted to cry over the sorrows, the indignities and the labors of his life. I shared all his pain—even that of his long, hopeless love for me; and I had but one wish—to alleviate his suffering.

"'My dear Lélio, my noble Rodrigue, my beautiful Don Juan!' I cried passionately.

"His eyes burned me. He spoke to me; he recounted every stage in the progression of his love for me; how from an actor of loose morals I had made of him a passionate, eager man, how I had raised him up in his own eyes, how I had given him back the courage and illusions of youth. He spoke to me of his respect, his veneration for me, of his scorn for the arrogant boasting of fashionable love; he told me he would give up the rest of his life for a single hour in my arms, but that he would sacrifice that hour and his life rather than offend me. Never has more persuasive eloquence won the heart of a woman; never did tender Racine speak with such conviction, such poetry, and such force. Everything delicate, profound, sweet, and impetuous that passion can inspire I learned from his words, his voice, his eyes, his caresses and his submission. Alas! Was he deluding himself? Was he playing a role?"

"No, I cannot believe he was!" I cried out, looking at the Marquise.

She seemed to grow younger as she spoke and to shed her eighty years like the fairy Urgele. As someone once said, the heart of a woman has no wrinkles.

"Listen to the rest," she said. "Lost, confused by all that he said to me, I threw my arms around him, thrilled as I touched the satin of his costume and smelled the perfume of his hair. I lost control. All that I was ignorant of, all that I thought myself incapable of feeling, was revealed to me; but it was too violent . . . I fainted . . .

"His prompt attention brought me back. I awoke to find him at my feet, more timid, more emotional than ever.

"'Take pity on me,' he said, 'kill me, drive me away.'

"He was paler and weaker than I.

"But the nervous turmoil that I had experienced in the course of this tumultuous day caused me to move quickly from one emotional state to another. The quick flash of a new existence had paled; I became calm again and the delicacy of true love took control.

"'Listen to me, Lélio,' I said to him, 'it is not contempt that tears me from your passion. It is possible that I possess all of the sensitivities that are instilled in us from childhood and that become like a second nature to us, but I would not be able to remember them because my very nature has just been transformed into another that I was not aware of before. If you love me, help me resist you. Let me leave here with the delicious satisfaction of having loved you with my heart alone. Perhaps, if I had never belonged to anyone, I could have given myself to you with joy, but understand that Larrieux has profaned me; understand that, driven by the horrible necessity to act like everyone else, I submitted to the caresses of a man whom I have never loved; understand that the disgust that I experienced so stifled my imagination that I would probably hate you now if I had succumbed to you a few moments ago. Let us not put ourselves to this terrible test! Stay pure in my heart and in my memory! Let us leave each other and keep forever our joyful thoughts and cherished memories. I swear, Lélio, that I will love you until I die. I know that the chill of age will not extinguish this ardent flame. And I swear never to give myself to another man after having resisted you. That will not be difficult for me, you can believe me.'

"Lélio prostrated himself before me; he did not implore me, he did not reproach me; he told me that he had not hoped for all the happiness that I had given him and that he did not have the right to ask for more. Nevertheless, as I heard his adieu, his despondency and the emotion in his voice alarmed me. I asked if he would not think of me with happiness; if the ecstasy of this night would not lavish its charm on all of his days; if his past and future suffering would not be lessened each time he invoked its memory. He revived himself to swear and promise all I asked. He fell again at my feet and kissed my dress with ardor. I felt unsteady; I made a sign and he withdrew. The carriage that I had requested arrived. The inscrutable attendant of this clandestine retreat knocked three times to alert me. Lélio threw himself in front of the door in despair: he looked like a spectre. I pushed him gently aside and he yielded. I went through the doorway and when he made a movement to follow me, I pointed to a chair in the middle of the salon beneath the statue of Isis. He sat down. An impassioned smile played across his lips; his eyes flashed a last look of gratitude and love. He was still handsome, still young, still a Spanish aristocrat. After a few steps, just as I was about to lose him forever, I turned and threw him one last look. Despair had broken him. He had become old, decayed, frightful once again. His body seemed paralyzed; his contracted lips attempted a distraught smile; his eyes were glazed and lifeless. He was only Lélio, the ghost of a lover and prince."

The Marquise paused; then with a somber smile, and as if she herself were decomposing like an old ruin that slowly crumbles, she continued:

"I have never heard of him since."

The Marquise paused again, longer this time than the first; but, with that dreadful strength of soul that results from long years, from the obstinate love of life or the hope of approaching death, she regained her cheerfulness and said to me, smiling:

"Well, now will you believe in virtue in the eighteenth century?"

"Madame," I replied, "I have no wish to doubt it; however, if I were less moved, perhaps I would tell you that you were lucky to have been bled that day."

"Miserable men!" exclaimed the Marquise. "You don't understand anything about matters of the heart!"

Notes

[1] In Corneille's classical tragedy *The Cid* (1836), the hero Rodrigue, an aristocrat, falls in love with Chimène and must prove that he is worthy of her. Corneille also wrote *Cinna* (1840).

[2] *Petite maisons,* secret trysting places, were popular in the eighteenth-century world of the aristocracy. Most libertine novels of the period—Chaderlos de Laclos's *Dangerous Liaisons*, for instance, mention these houses.

[3] Racine's tragedy *Bajazet* (1672) deals with a Turkish sultan. In Racine's *Phèdre* (1677), based on a Greek myth, the queen falls madly in love with her stepson, *Hippolyte*, son of the Greek king Thésée.

[4] Claire-Joseph Léris, known as Clairon (1723–1803), was a French actress famous for her roles in Voltaire's plays.

[5] Molière's classical play *Dom Juan ou le festin de Pierre* (1665). For a discussion of George Sand's use of the Don Juan theme, see Béatrice Didier, "George Sand et *Don Giovanni*," *Revue des Sciences Humaines* 226 (Avril–Juin 1992), 37–53.

◆ | *Pauline* | ◆

⋄ I ⋄

Three years ago in Saint-Front, an ugly little town that you won't find on any map, something happened that caused quite a stir. It wasn't particularly interesting and few people heard of it, but it had serious consequences.

One dark, cold and rainy night, a postchaise entered the courtyard of the Auberge du Lion Couronné. A woman's voice demanded fresh horses: "Quickly, quickly!" The postilion reluctantly approached and replied that that was easier said than done; there weren't any horses because the epidemic (the same epidemic that seems to plague all post houses on less traveled roads) had claimed thirty-seven horses just last week. He added that the travelers might still continue on later that night, but they would have to wait until the team had rested a bit.

"Will it be long?" asked the footman, wrapped in fur in the coachman's box.

"About an hour," replied the postilion, his boots still half off. "We'll give 'em some oats right away."

The footman swore. A pretty young chambermaid, her head swathed in a confusion of scarves, appeared at the coach door. She mumbled a mild complaint about the exhaustion and boredom of traveling. The lady escorted by these two servants now stepped gingerly down onto the cold wet paving stones, shook her sable-lined cloak, and set off toward the kitchen without uttering a word.

She was a young woman, strikingly beautiful, but pale from fatigue. She declined the offer of a room and, while her servants chose to shut themselves up in the coach to sleep, she sat before the hearth in a classic coach-house chair, that harsh intractable refuge of uncomplaining travelers. The servant on duty went back to snoring, her body folded across a bench, her head resting on the table. The cat, who had been displaced against his will to make way for the traveler, curled up again near the warm cinders. For several moments, he fixed his glowing green eyes on the newcomer with a look of scorn and distrust, but his pupils slowly contracted again, until they became only a thin black line on an emerald background. He returned to his habitual self-centered satisfaction, rounding his back and purring in smug complacency. In fact, he ended up falling asleep between the paws of a large dog who had found a way to co-exist peacefully with him, thanks to the perpetual concessions that, for the good of society, the weak extract from the strong.

The traveler tried in vain to fall asleep. A thousand images filled her dreams, and she woke with a start. The sort of childish memories that haunt active imaginations crowded her brain and wearied her, until at last one dominant thought overshadowed them all.

"Yes, it was a dreary town," thought the traveler. "A town with dark, angular streets, roughly paved. A poor, ugly little town, like this one, as it appeared to me just now through the mist that covered my carriage windows. Only here there are one or two, maybe even three, street lamps, but in that town, there wasn't a single one. Everyone on foot carried a lantern after curfew. It was a wretched, awful little town, and yet I spent vigorous years of my youth there. I was very different then . . . poor in circumstance but rich in energy and hope. How I suffered! My life was anonymous and plagued by inactivity; but who can give me back that eager soul tormented by its own energies? Oh, my heart's youth, whatever became of you . . . ?"

Then, after this somewhat grandiloquent address of the sort that impassioned minds sometimes vent at destiny, without much reason perhaps, but from some innate need to dramatize their existence in their own eyes, the young woman smiled involuntarily, as if some inner voice had answered that she was still happy; and she tried to fall asleep, waiting for the hour to pass.

The kitchen of the inn was lit only by an iron lantern suspended from the ceiling. The frame of the lantern threw a trembling network of shadows across the entire room as it cast a pale light on the smoke-blackened beams of the ceiling.

Because of the darkness, the stranger had entered the room without noticing her surroundings; moreover, her fatigue prevented her from remarking anything particular about the place.

Suddenly, the movement of a small avalanche of cinders revealed two half-burned logs still lit with a melancholy glow. A small flame flickered, darted up, waned, shot forth again, and grew bright enough to illuminate the entire hearth. The listless eyes of the traveler, mechanically following this movement of light, stopped suddenly on a pale inscription reflected against the darkened mantelpiece of the fireplace. She started, rubbed her sleep-heavy eyes, picked up a flaming stick to examine the letters, and then let it fall again, crying out with emotion:

"My God, where am I? Is this a dream?"

At this outburst, the servant awoke suddenly and, turning toward her, asked if she had called.

"Yes, yes," cried the stranger. "Come here. Tell me, who wrote these two names on the wall?"

"Two names?" the servant repeated, dumbfounded. "What names?"

"Oh!" cried the stranger, speaking to herself excitedly, "Her name and mine, Pauline, Laurence! And this date! February 10, 182 . . . ! Oh! Tell me, tell me, why are these names and this date here?"

"Madame," replied the servant, "I have never paid any attention to them, and, anyway, I don't know how to read."

"But where am I then? What's the name of this town? Isn't it Villiers, the first stop after I . . . ?"

"Oh, no, Madame; you're in Saint-Front, on the road to Paris, at the Auberge du Lion Couronné."

"Heavens!" cried the traveler warmly as she leaped up.

The terrified servant thought the stranger was mad and tried to leave; but the young woman stopped her, crying:

"Please stay, and talk to me! How did I come to be here? Tell me, am I dreaming? If I am, wake me!"

"Madame, you're not dreaming, nor am I, I think," replied the servant. "You intended to go to Lyon? Well, you must have forgotten to tell the postilion, and, quite naturally, he would have thought you were going to Paris. These days, the relay coaches all go to Paris."

"But I told him myself that I was going to Lyon."

"Well then, it's because Baptiste is too deaf to hear a cannon, and what's more, he's asleep on his horse half the time and his animals are accustomed to taking the road to Paris these days . . ."

"Saint Front!" repeated the stranger. "What strange fate brings me back to the place I had hoped to avoid? I took a detour to avoid coming here, and, because I fell asleep for two hours, chance led me here without my knowledge. Well, perhaps God wanted it so. Let me find out what joy or sorrow awaits me here. Tell me, my dear," she added, addressing the maidservant of the inn, "do you know of a Mademoiselle Pauline D— in this town?"

I don't know anyone here, Madame," replied the girl. "I've only been here a week."

"Well, find me another servant, then! I want to know if she's here. Since I'm here after all, I want to know everything. Is she married? Is she dead? Go on, go on, find out for me; hurry!"

The maid objected that all the servants were asleep, and that the stable boy and the postilions didn't know anyone but their horses. A quick show of generosity on the part of the young woman prompted the maid to go and wake up the cook. After a fifteen-minute delay, which seemed interminable to our traveler, the servant returned to inform her that Mademoiselle Pauline D— was not married and was still living in the town. The young woman immediately requested that her coach be put in the coach-house and that a room be prepared for her.

She went to bed to await the dawn, but she couldn't sleep. Memories that she had long forgotten or kept at bay crowded in on her; she now recognized everything she had laid eyes upon at the Auberge du Lion Couronné. Even though the ancient inn had improved considerably over the past ten years, the furniture remained essentially the same. The walls were still covered with tapestries copied from *L'Astrée*'s most beautiful scenes; the shepherdesses' faces had been mended with white thread, and ragged shepherds floated, suspended by nails that pierced their chests. There was a Roman soldier's ghastly portrait drawn by the innkeeper's daughter, and framed with four pieces of black wood. On the fireplace, a manger scene with wax figures was yellowing under a glass canopy.

"Alas!" thought the traveler, "I remember spending several days in this very room twelve years ago,* when I first arrived here with my dear mother! I watched her waste away in poverty, and almost lost her in this dreary town. I slept in this very bed the night before I left! What a night of suffering, hope, regret and expectation! How my dear friend, my sweet Pauline, wept as she kissed me in front of the fireplace where I was dozing earlier without realizing where I was! How I cried too, as I etched her name under mine on the wall, with the date of our separation! Poor Pauline! What has her life been like since? The life of a provincial old maid! How horrible! She was so loving, so superior to everything around her! And yet, I wanted to run away from her, I promised myself that I would never see her again! Still, I might bring her some consolation, one day of joy in her life! But, what if she rejects me! What if she has been overcome by prejudice! ... Alas! That's surely the case. How can I have any doubts? Didn't she stop writing as soon as she learned of the decision

---

* There is some confusion in the time sequence here. If Laurence had spent four years in St Front before leaving ten years ago, she would have been in that room fourteen years earlier, not twelve.

I had made? She must have feared that she would be corrupted or degraded if she stayed in contact with someone like me! Oh! Pauline! She loved me so, and yet she was ashamed of me . . . ! I don't know what to think any more. . . . Now that I find myself so close to her, now that I'm sure to find her again in the same circumstances in which I knew her, I can't resist the desire to see her. Oh! I *shall* see her, even if she rejects me! If she does, let the shame be hers! I have overcome my fears, I have honored our pledges of the past, and she has disavowed them!"

In the midst of these thoughts, she saw the cold gray morning creep from behind the uneven roofs of the neglected houses leaning awkwardly against each other. She recognized the steeple that used to mark her hours of rest or reverie; she saw the townfolk awaking beneath their traditional cotton nightcaps; and their ancient faces, faintly familiar, as they appeared sullenly at the street windows. She heard the blacksmith's anvil ring behind the walls of a crumbling house; she saw farmers in blue cloaks and oilcloth headdresses arriving at the market; everything was falling into place and looked just as it had in the past. Each of these insignificant details made the traveler's heart beat harder even though it all seemed horribly poor and ugly to her.

"What!" she exclaimed. "I managed to spend four years here, four whole years without dying! I breathed this air, talked to these people, slept under these moss-covered roofs and walked down these muddy streets! And Pauline, my poor Pauline, still lives in the midst of all this. She was so beautiful, so likeable, so well educated that she could have risen and reigned as I have in the brilliance and luxury of high society!"

When the town clock chimed seven, she hastily finished dressing; and, while her servants were cursing the inn and suffering the inconvenience of travel with the characteristic impatience and haughtiness of wealthy household staff, she hurried down the winding streets on tiptoe with the grace of a Parisian, and was greeted with astonished stares by the townsfolk, for whom an unknown face was a major event.

Pauline's house was by no means attractive, although it was quite old. It had retained from the period of its origin only its dampness and its inconvenient design; not a single unusual or elegant architectural feature remained, not the slightest trace of medieval romantic appeal. Everything about it seemed somber and sorrowful, from the copper face etched on the doorknocker, to the equally ugly and sullen face of the elderly servant who opened the door, looked at the stranger with disdain and then turned her back to her, announcing curtly: "She's here."

The traveler felt at once exhilarated and torn as she climbed the spiral staircase, for which a worn rope served as banister. This house reminded her of her early life, the purest scenes of her youth; but when she compared these ghosts from her past to the luxury of her current life, she couldn't help feeling sorry for Pauline, who was condemned to vegetate here like the greenish moss that crept up the damp walls.

She quietly climbed the stairs and silently pushed open the door. Nothing had changed in the large room, grandly entitled "the parlor" by its owners. The same reddish tiled floor, impeccably clean, the spotless brown woodwork; the mirror with its once gilded frame; the massive furniture, finely embroidered by some family ancestor; and two or three religious paintings left by an uncle, the town priest. Everything had remained in precisely the same spot and in the same ancient and solid state for more than ten years, ten years during which the stranger seemed to have lived a century! So, everything she saw appeared to her like a dream.

The impression of darkness and depth created by the vast, low-ceilinged room was not without charm. There was a feeling of austerity and meditation, as in some of Rembrandt's paintings, where one can make out, in the dim light, the wrinkled face of a philoso-pher or an alchemist, brown and earthy like the walls, stark and sickly like the cleverly planned ray of light in which it floats. A window with narrow panes of leaded glass, decorated with pots of geraniums and basil, was the only source of light in this vast space; yet a sweet face shone in the light of the window re-cess and seemed positioned there, as if by design, so that the beauty of the face would stand out alone within the picture. It was Pauline.

She had changed a great deal, and, since the traveler couldn't see the details of her face, she wondered for some time whether it was indeed her friend. When Laurence had left, Pauline was shorter by a full head, and now she was tall and so exceedingly thin that she seemed in danger of breaking when she moved. She was dressed in brown, with a perfectly pleated white collar, like a monk's. Her beautiful auburn hair was carefully combed back flat against her temples; she was immersed in a classic task, obviously boring to any thinking mind: doing minute embroidery with an imperceptible needle on a bit of cloth, counting each thread. The lives of more than half the women in France are wasted on this solemn occupation.

After the traveler had taken a few steps, she could distinguish the lines of Pauline's beautiful profile in the light of the window: her calm, regular features, her large, veiled, unemotional eyes, her smooth, pure forehead, enlarged by her pulled-back hair, and her delicate mouth, which seemed incapable of smiling. She was still wonderfully attractive, but too thin and chronically pale. At first glance, her old friend was tempted to pity her; but as she admired the profound serenity of this melancholy brow gently bent over the embroidery, she felt herself moved more by respect than by pity.

She remained silent and motionless, staring at her for quite a while; but suddenly, as if Pauline had instinctively sensed her presence through some movement of the heart, the young woman turned towards

Laurence and stared at her without uttering a word and without changing expression.

"Pauline, don't you recognize me?" cried the stranger. "Have you forgotten Laurence's face?"

Pauline uttered a cry, stood up and then fell back in her chair. Laurence flew into her arms and both of them were weeping.

"You didn't recognize me?" Laurence finally asked.

"How can you say that?" Pauline replied. "I recognized you, but I wasn't surprised. You see, Laurence, people who lead solitary lives sometimes have strange thoughts. How can I explain? Memories, images, crowd their minds and appear to pass before their eyes. My mother calls them hallucinations. But I know I'm not crazy. I just think that God allows people I love to appear in my daydreams, to make up for my isolation. In fact, I have often seen you in the doorway, standing as you used to do, and watching me hesitantly. I have developed the habit of staying silent and motionless, so that the vision will not disappear. I was startled only when I heard you speak. Then your voice woke me! It knocked directly at my heart! Dear Laurence! Is it truly you? Tell me it's you!"

When Laurence timidly explained to her friend the fear that had for years prevented her from making contact, Pauline embraced her, crying.

"Oh, dear," she said, "you thought that I despised you, that I was ashamed of you! I who have always had the highest respect for you, and who knew that whatever the circumstances, a soul like yours could never go astray."

Laurence blushed and then paled at hearing these words from her friend; she held back a sigh, and kissed Pauline's hand reverently.

"It's certainly true," Pauline continued, "that your present circumstances shock the narrow and intolerant minds of everyone here. The only person who still seems to feel some affection and regret in spite of her disapproval is my mother. She does blame you, as you must expect; but she tries to excuse you, and it's obviously painful for her to condemn you. She's not very open-minded, as you know, but the poor woman does have a kind heart!"

"How can I get her to see me then?" Laurence asked.

"Alas!" Pauline answered. "It would be easy to deceive her; she is blind."

"Blind? Oh! My Lord!"

Laurence was devastated by the news; and when she thought of Pauline's horrible existence, she regarded her with deep respect and compassion. Pauline understood, and pressed her hand tenderly, saying with touching naïveté:

"There is some good in every misfortune God sends us. I almost got married five years ago; a year later, my mother lost her sight. How fortunate, you see, that I was still single and able to care for her! Had I been married, who knows if I could have?"

Laurence, in deep admiration, felt her eyes well with tears.

"Obviously," she told her friend, smiling through her tears, "you would have been distracted by a thousand other concerns, and she would have been much worse off than she is now."

"I hear her stirring," Pauline said.

And she swiftly moved to the adjoining room, careful not to make any noise.

Laurence tiptoed after her, and saw the blind old woman lying on a bed shaped like a bier. Her skin was an oily yellow. Her wasted, lifeless eyes made her look exactly like a corpse. Laurence, struck by instinctive terror, stepped back. Pauline walked towards her mother, leaned her own face gently over that hideous one, and asked her in a whisper whether she was sleeping. The blind woman did not reply and turned towards the other side of her bed. Pauline carefully straightened the blankets over her emaciated limbs, quietly closed the bed curtain, and led her friend back to the parlor.

"Let's chat," she said; "my mother usually gets up late. We have a few hours to get reacquainted; we'll have to find a way to rekindle her old feelings for you. Perhaps all we need to do is tell her you're here! But please tell me, Laurence, how could you have thought that I—Oh! I can't say the word!—despised you! How insulting for me! But I suppose it's my fault. I should have guessed that you would doubt my love for you, I should have explained my reasons. . . . Alas! It would have been so difficult to make you understand! You would have accused me of being weak when it took enormous strength to give up writing to you, and not to follow you into that unknown world where my heart has gone so many times to look for you in spite of myself! And I didn't dare blame my mother; I couldn't bring myself to reveal her narrow-mindedness and prejudices to you. I was victimized by them; but I was ashamed to talk about it. When one is so isolated from all friendship, so alone, so sad, a difficult step becomes an impossible one. We observe ourselves, become afraid of our emotions, commit suicide for fear of withering away. Now that you're here with me again, my confidence, my trust are returning. I'll tell you everything. But first, let's talk about you, for my life is so monotonous, so empty, so pale compared to yours! You must have so many things to tell me!"

The reader must assume that Laurence did not tell everything. Her tale, in fact, was much shorter than Pauline had expected. We will summarize it here in a few lines.

First, it should be said that Laurence was born in Paris in modest circumstances. She received a simple but sound education. She was fifteen when her family became destitute, and she had to leave Paris and retire to the country with her mother. She came to Saint-Front, where she managed to live for four years as a teacher's assistant in a girls' boarding school, and where she developed a close friendship with her oldest pupil, Pauline, who was also fifteen.

And then, through the sponsorship of one dowager or another, Laurence was called back to Paris to educate a banker's daughters.

If you wish to know how a young woman seeks and discovers her vocation, how she pursues it in spite of every objection and obstacle, you can reread the charming memoirs of Mademoiselle Hippolyte Clairon, a famous actress of the eighteenth century.

Laurence did what all predestined artists do: she suffered through all the misery, all the agony of unrecognized, unappreciated talent. Finally, having endured all the vicissitudes of the artist's life, she became a beautiful and intelligent actress. Success, riches, respect, fame: all came to her suddenly and simultaneously. From that moment on, she enjoyed a brilliant career and the respect which people of intelligence believe is due to genuine talent and nobility of character. She did not tell Pauline of her mistakes, her passions, her sorrows as a woman, her disappointments and her regrets. It was still too soon: Pauline wouldn't have understood.

⬩ II ⬩

By the time the blind woman awoke at noon, Pauline knew all there was to know about Laurence's life, even what had not been told, and that was perhaps the most important. People who live in a calm retreat have a marvelous instinct for imagining storms and disasters in other people's lives, and they secretly rejoice at having avoided them themselves. It is a consolation that must be allowed these people, since pride, too, has its needs, and virtue alone cannot always compensate for long hours of boredom and solitude.

"Well," said the blind mother, sitting up on the edge of the bed and leaning against her daughter, "who is here with us? I can smell the perfume of an elegant lady. I'll bet it's Madame Ducornay, back from Paris with all sorts of beautiful clothes that I won't be able to see, and wearing one of those strong perfumes that always give us headaches."

"No, Mother, it isn't Madame Ducornay," Pauline answered.

"Who then?" the blind woman persisted, reaching out her hand.

"Guess," Pauline said, signaling Laurence to touch the old woman's hand.

"What a soft little hand!" cried the blind woman, stroking the actress's hand with her knotty fingers. "Oh! This certainly can't be Madame Ducornay. It can't be one of our 'grandes dames' because, whatever they try, one can always recognize the hare by the paw. Yet, I know this hand. It belongs to someone I haven't seen for a long time. Won't she speak?"

"My voice has changed, like my hand," Laurence replied. Theatrical training had given a deeper, more sonorous tone to her naturally clear, fresh voice.

"I know this voice too, but I'm not sure I can identify it," said the blind woman.

She remained silent for a moment, without releasing Laurence's hand, her dull, glassy eyes raised towards the young woman's face in a frightening stare.

"Can she see me?" Laurence whispered to Pauline.

"Not at all," the latter replied; "but her memory is excellent; and besides, our lives are so uneventful, she will certainly realize who you are in a moment."

Pauline had hardly uttered these words when the blind woman thrust Laurence's hand from her in horror and disgust, and cried in a harsh, broken voice:

"Oh! That wretched actress! What is she doing here? You shouldn't have let her in, Pauline!"

"Oh, Mother!" Pauline cried, blushing in shame and sorrow, and holding her mother close so that the old woman could feel her emotion.

Laurence grew pale, but quickly regained her composure:

"I was expecting this," she told Pauline with a gentle, dignified smile that surprised and troubled her friend.

"Never mind," continued the blind woman, who instinctively feared displeasing the daughter whose devotion was so essential to her. "Give me a moment to collect myself; I was so surprised! And one doesn't always know what one is saying when first awakening . . . I wouldn't want to hurt your feelings, Mademoiselle . . . or Madame . . . What do they call you now?"

"Laurence, as always," the actress answered calmly.

"She's still the same Laurence," Pauline exclaimed with warmth and kindness, giving her friend a kiss. "She still has the same generous soul, the same noble heart. . . ."

"Come, Daughter, help me get dressed," said the blind woman, changing the subject, unable to decide whether to contradict her daughter or to reconcile with Laurence. "Comb my hair, Pauline; I forget that others aren't blind and can see how awful I look. Give me my veil and my tippet. . . . Good, and now bring me my hot chocolate, and offer some to this . . . lady."

Pauline gave her friend an imploring look, and the latter replied with a kiss. When the old woman, wrapped in a cloak of brown calico with large red flowers and wearing a white bonnet topped with a black veil that half hid her face, was settled in front of her frugal lunch, she softened a bit. Age, boredom and infirmity had made her so selfish that she would sacrifice anything, even the most deeply held prejudices, to secure her personal comfort. Any distraction or vexation on her daughter's part threatened to disrupt the series of innumerable small attentions that the old woman required from her to make life bearable. Only when the blind woman was settled in bed for the night, and no longer feared any danger or deprivation, would she allow herself the perverse comfort of insulting the person she no longer needed with bitter words and unjust complaints. At her hours of need, she knew very well how to contain herself and maintain her daughter's zeal with a more pleasant manner. Laurence observed all this at her leisure in the course of the day. She noticed something else which saddened her even more: the old woman was deeply afraid of her daughter. It seemed that through all of her admirable sacrifice, Pauline unwittingly harbored a silent but constant grudge, one that her mother understood very well and feared terribly. These two women were afraid to reveal to each other their mutual weariness at being constantly together, one a step away from death, the other in the prime of life. One feared the actions of the other which could at any moment steal her final breath; the other was terrified of the grave into which this living cadaver threatened to drag her.

Laurence, in her compassionate wisdom, told herself that it had to be this way, and that the inescapable suffering of Pauline didn't detract from her patience, but rather enhanced her worth. Yet, in spite of these thoughts, Laurence sensed that she herself was gripped by fear and ennui in the presence of these two victims. She felt a cloud pass over her eyes, and a chill through her veins. By evening, she was exhausted, even though she had done nothing the entire day. The horror of reality displaced the poetic vision that she, with her artist's eye, had first imposed on Pauline's saintly existence. She would have liked to maintain her illusion, and believe Pauline radiantly happy in her martyrdom, like a medieval Catholic virgin, and believe that her mother was contented as well, forgetting her misery and thinking only of the joy of being loved and cared for in this way. In short, if she had to witness this somber domestic scene, she would have preferred to have it peopled with angels of light rather than these cold, sorrowful figures drawn from reality. The slightest wrinkle on Pauline's angelic face cast a shadow on Laurence's vision; an unkind word from this pure mouth disrupted the mysterious gentleness that Laurence had at first seen shining there. And yet Pauline's frown was like a prayer; the word that escaped her lips was an expression of consolation and solicitude. But all of it was as cold as Christian selfishness, which makes us bear anything in the hope of a reward, and as barren as monastic renunciation, which forbids us to ease the burden of other people's lives or our own.

As the actress's naïvely enthusiastic admiration waned, the two bourgeois women just as naïvely were undergoing the opposite metamorphosis in spite of themselves. While Pauline had often shuddered at the thought of the luxurious society into which her friend had thrown herself, she nevertheless unconsciously felt a great curiosity about this unknown, glamorous and terrifying world which her principles forbade her to explore. Upon seeing Laurence, admiring her beauty, her grace, her demeanor, at times as regal as a queen's, at times as free and playful as a child's (for a celebrated actress is like a child who considers the whole world her family), Pauline felt within her the blossoming of an exhilarating and unsettling emotion, something between admiration and fear, tenderness and envy.

As for the blind woman, she was entranced, enlivened by the beauty of Laurence's voice, by the purity of her language, and by her wit. The young woman possessed that lively, natural intelligence that characterizes true artists, particularly in the theatrical world. Pauline's mother, despite her religious beliefs and provincial arrogance, was a more astute and educated woman than might be expected in her circumstances. She was delighted, in spite of herself, at an encounter so different from, and so superior to, anything she had experienced before. She may not have quite realized it herself, but Laurence's efforts to overcome her prejudices were entirely successful. The old woman was beginning to enjoy the actress's conversation so much that when she heard their guest ask for post-horses, she reacted with a regret that bordered on panic. She begged Laurence to stay another day. The young woman hesitated and then agreed. Her own mother had been detained in Paris by her younger sister's illness, and had not been able to accompany her.

Laurence had been obliged to leave because of her agreement with the theater in Orléans. She had arranged to meet her family in Lyon, and wanted to arrive when they did, because she knew that after a two-week separation (their first ever), they would be impatiently awaiting her. However, the blind woman insisted so strongly, and Pauline wept so sincerely at the thought of losing her friend once again, and possibly forever, that Laurence assented. She wrote her mother, telling her not to worry if she arrived in Lyon a day late and requested that the horses be ready the following evening. The blind woman, more and more entranced, even went so far as to send a friendly note to her former acquaintance, Laurence's mother.

"Poor Madame S——," she remarked, when she heard the letter being folded and sealed with wax, "she was really an excellent person, witty, merry, trusting . . . yet very careless! For, after all, my poor child, she will have to answer to God for your unfortunate decision to go on the stage. She could have opposed it, and yet she didn't! I wrote her three letters at the time. God only knows whether she read them! Oh, if she had only listened to me, you wouldn't be where you are now! . . ."

"We would have been destitute," Laurence answered with a quiet intensity, "and we would have suffered from not being able to help each other, whereas today I have the joy of seeing my dear mother grow young again surrounded by modest luxury. And she is even happier than I, if possible, because she owes her well-being to my work and my perseverance. Oh! She is a wonderful mother, my dear Madame D——, and even though I am an actress, I can assure you that I love her as much as Pauline loves you."

"You always were a good daughter, I know," replied the blind woman. "But how will all of this end? You are well off, which your mother appreciates, because she always loved her comfort and pleasures, but neither of you thinks of the afterlife! . . . Still, I console myself with the thought that you will not always remain in the theatre, and the day will come when you will repent."

In the meantime, the news of an adventure which had brought a lady in a post-chaise to Saint-Front on the Paris road, when she thought she was going to Villiers on the road to Lyon, had been racing through the small town and, for the past several hours, had given rise to wild speculation. What fate, what luck, could cause this same lady to stay another whole day, after having arrived by accident? And what in heaven's name was she doing at the Dames D——'s home? How could she have been acquainted with them? And what could they have to say to each other, shut up together for so long? The town clerk, who was playing billiards at the café directly across the street from the D—'s, had seen, or was believed to have seen, this unusual woman, unusually and even magnificently dressed, according to him, pace back and forth before the windows of the house. Laurence's travel attire was in reality quite simple and in good taste; but a Parisian, and a female artist in particular, can dazzle provincials with the slightest finery.

All the women in the neighborhood were glued to their windows, even pushing them open and catching cold, in the hope of finding out what was happening at their neighbors' house. They hailed the servant on her way to market and questioned her. She knew nothing, wouldn't answer, didn't understand a thing; but, according to her, the person in question was very odd. She paced with huge strides, spoke in a gruff voice, and wore a fur-lined cloak that made her look like an animal from a traveling menagerie, either a lioness or a tigress, the servant could not quite decide which. The town clerk decided that she must be wearing a panther's skin, and the assistant to the mayor thought that she must be the Duchess of Berry. He had always suspected the old D— of being a legitimist at heart, because of her piety.

The mayor, plagued with questions by his womenfolk, found a marvelous excuse to satisfy their curiosity and his own. He ordered the postmaster not to deliver the stranger her horses without first seeing her passport. However, when the stranger delayed her departure until the next day, she had her servant inform the postmaster that she would show her passport when she came to claim the horses. The servant, a clever fellow, was amused by the curiosity of the people of Saint-Front, and chose to tell each of them a different tale. Hence, a thousand versions of the story circulated and collided in the streets. Minds were set afire; the mayor feared an uprising; the king's procurator asked the police to be on alert, and police mounts were saddled and held ready the entire day.

"What can we do?" wondered the mayor, who was a peaceful man with a soft spot for the weaker sex. "I can't possibly send a policeman to impudently examine a lady's papers!"

"I wouldn't hesitate if I were you!" boomed the deputy public prosecutor, a fierce young magistrate who hoped to become the king's procurator, and who constantly struggled to lose weight in order to resemble Junius Brutus.

"You wouldn't want me to act precipitously!" the peaceful magistrate replied.

The mayor's wife took counsel with the other wives, and it was decided that Monsieur le Maire would go in person and, in the most polite manner possible, apologize for having to obey higher orders and ask the stranger for her passport.

The mayor obeyed, while taking care not to reveal that the higher orders were from his wife. Madame D— was a bit puzzled by the request; Pauline, who understood quite well, was worried and hurt; Laurence only laughed, called the mayor by his first name, and asked him about his entire family, recalling with prodigious memory the oldest to the youngest of his children. She led him on for a while, and then finally revealed who she was. She was so charming and so delightful throughout this banter that the good mayor fell madly in love with her, asked to kiss her hand, and departed only after Madame D— and Pauline had invited him to dine that very evening with the beautiful actress *from Paris*.

The dinner was quite gay. Laurence tried to forget her dismal first impression, and decided to reward the blind woman with a few hours of merriment for having given up her prejudices. She recounted dozens of tales about her travels in the provinces and, during dessert, even consented to recite some classical verse for Monsieur le Maire, which caused him such ecstasy that Madame la Mairesse would surely have been jealous. Never in her life had the blind woman had such a good time. Pauline was strangely upset; she was surprised to feel sad in the midst of her joy. Laurence, in wishing to entertain the others, had begun to enjoy herself. She felt ten years younger in this world of her memories that she occasionally still inhabited in her dreams.

They had left the dining room for the parlor and were finishing their coffee when the sound of wooden shoes on the staircase announced an incoming visitor. It was the mayor's wife, who could no longer contain her curiosity and cleverly pretended to drop in for a visit with Madame D——. She had been careful not to bring her daughters, for fear they would damage their marriage prospects by laying eyes on an actress. As a result, her daughters stayed awake the entire night; never in their lives had maternal authority seemed so unjust. The youngest cried with vexation.

Madame la Mairesse, unsure of what sort of welcome to give Laurence (who had tutored her daughters years ago), made an effort not to be rude. She even grew gracious when she observed Laurence's air of calm dignity. But minutes later a second visitor arrived, also "by chance," and the mayoress moved back her chair and spoke less to the actress. She was being watched by one of her intimate friends who would surely have criticized her familiarity with a stage actress. This second visitor had also vowed to satisfy her curiosity by chatting with Laurence. But, in addition to the fact that Laurence was becoming increasingly serious and reserved, the presence of the mayoress constrained and thwarted the second visitor's curiosity. The third visitor disturbed the first two a great deal, and she in turn became even more uncomfortable with the arrival of a fourth visitor. Indeed, in less than an hour, Pauline's ancient parlor was packed as if she had invited the entire town to a gala event. No one could resist; they all craved, even at the risk of doing something strange or impolite, a glimpse of this former governess whose intelligence no one had suspected, and who was now known and sought after across France. To legitimize their curiosity and to excuse the lack of judgment they had shown in the past, they pretended to doubt Laurence's talent and whispered to one another:

"Is it really true that she is a friend and protegée of Mademoiselle Mars?" "They say she is immensely successful in Paris!" "Do you really think that's possible?" "We've heard that the most celebrated authors write plays for her." "Perhaps all of this has been greatly exaggerated!" "Have you talked to her?" "Do you ever see her?" and so forth.

But none of these doubts could diminish Laurence's grace and beauty. Just before dinner, she called for her chambermaid and—from a tiny case that resembled one of those enchanted nuts from which fairies, with the wave of a magic wand, make an entire princess's wardrobe appear—she drew out a very simple exquisitely tasteful dress, marvelously fresh. Pauline could not understand how someone could transform herself while travelling with so little time and trouble: her friend's elegance made her dizzy. The local ladies had looked forward to criticizing the clothes and appearance that had been pronounced so strange; yet they were forced to admire the soft, sumptuous material, the elegant style,

neither stiff nor showy. An elegant woman of the provinces can never successfully emulate her city counter-
part, even by copying her exactly. The refinement of
shoes, cuffs and hairdos is either absurdly exaggerated
or shabbily neglected. What was more striking and in-
timidating than anything else was Laurence's complete
ease and genuine elegance that in the provinces was
not expected in a stage actress, and that was certainly
not to be found in any of the women of Saint-Front.
Laurence was imperious and gracious at will. She
smiled to herself at the discomfort she was causing these
narrow minds who had come, each without knowing
about the others, thinking herself the only one brave
enough to make fun of this bohemian's improprieties.
Now, here they all were, ashamed and embarrassed by
the presence of the others, and even worse, disappointed
at feeling envious of what they had come to ridicule!
All the women sat on one side of the drawing room
like a regiment in flight, while Laurence, like an af-
fable queen who smiles at her subjects and yet keeps
them at a distance, sat on the other, surrounded by
Pauline, her mother and a few sensible men who were
not afraid to chat respectfully with her. Roles had been
reversed, and while awkwardness increased on one side,
true dignity triumphed on the other. They no longer
dared to whisper, nor even to stare, except for an occasional glance. Finally, when the departure of the most
disappointed thinned the ranks, the women ventured
to draw closer, beg for a word, a glance, touch her dress,

ask for her seamstress's address, the price of her jewelry, the name of the most fashionable plays in Paris, and request theatre tickets for their first trip to the capital.

With the arrival of visitors, the blind woman was initially confused, then annoyed, then hurt. As she heard all these people fill her cold drawing room, empty for so long, she decided not to be ashamed of her friendship with Laurence; she became even more affectionate toward the young woman, and greeted the visitors with biting irony.

"Yes indeed, my dears," she chirped, "I must be in better health than I thought, because people are no longer put off by my decrepitude. It's been two years since anyone has paid me an evening visit; it's a marvelous stroke of luck that the whole town decided to come at once. Has the calendar been changed and could this be my saint's day, the one I thought I celebrated six months ago?" Then, addressing others who had hardly ever visited her house, she inquired sardonically:

"Ah! You're just like me, you forget your scruples and come in spite of it all to pay homage to talent? It's always like that, you see; wit conquers all! You blamed Mademoiselle S— for having launched a theatrical career. You were just like me, I say, you thought it was revolting, horrible! And yet here you are at her feet! You can't deny it, because I don't believe for a moment that I've become interesting enough to draw such a crowd to my door."

As for Pauline, she had always entertained warm feelings for her friend. She had never been ashamed of their friendship and, with truly heroic courage for a provincial girl, she had braved the petty criticisms leveled at her, and now chose to be as friendly with Laurence in public as she was in private. She showered her friend with attention, kindness and respect; she thoughtfully placed a stool under Laurence's feet. She offered her refreshments; then she embraced her effusively after Laurence thanked her with a kiss; and when Pauline at last sat down next to Laurence's chair, she held on to her hand for the rest of the evening.

It was an attractive role to be sure, and Laurence's presence had worked miracles, for a day earlier such courageous acts would have terrified Pauline. Now her strength surprised her. If she had examined her soul, she might have discovered that this generous role was the only one that could raise her to Laurence's level in her own eyes. Up to that point, the actress's grace, nobility and intelligence had disconcerted her a little; but now that she was posing as Laurence's protegée, her friend's superiority no longer disturbed her, despite the difficulty we all experience when we find ourselves in an inferior position.

When the two friends were finally left alone again by the fire with the blind woman, it pained and surprised Pauline to hear her friend direct all her praise and gratitude to her mother. The actress kissed Madame D—'s hand with genuine deference as she helped her to her room and expressed her appreciation for the old woman's handling of the ordeal.

"As for you, Pauline," she told her friend when they were left alone once again, "I wouldn't dream of offending you with praise. Since you hold no prejudices, it isn't difficult for you to reject this provincial narrow-mindedness and stupidity. I know you, you couldn't be yourself without taking real pleasure in rising above such pettiness."

"You make it a joy," Pauline replied, somewhat reluctantly.

"Well, now, be truthful!" cried Laurence with a kiss. "You acted in good conscience, didn't you?"

Was it ungrateful for Pauline's friend to speak like this? No. Laurence was always very fair with others and completely true to herself. If her friend's efforts had seemed extraordinary to her, she would have shown her gratitude without hesitation. But since she herself had so strong and legitimate a sense of her own dignity, she truly believed Pauline's courage to be as natural and easy as her own. She had no inkling of the secret anguish that she had kindled in this troubled soul. She could not imagine it; and if she had, she would not have understood it.

Pauline, who didn't want to leave her even for a moment, asked Laurence to sleep in her bed. She had a large sofa prepared for herself nearby, so that she could chat with Laurence as long as possible. The young recluse's restlessness grew steadily, as did her desire to understand the wider world, the pleasures of artistic life and fame, of being an active and independent woman. Laurence deflected her questions. She thought it unwise for Pauline to explore the attractions of circumstances so different from her own. Indeed, Laurence tried not to paint an attractive picture of her life. She responded to Pauline's questions with other questions, attempting to get her friend to describe the private joys of her own saintly life and to discuss the beauty and pleasures of dutiful devotion which, she thought, must surely be the reward of a pious and devoted soul. But Pauline answered with great reluctance. During their early morning chat, she had exhausted all her pride and graciousness in hiding her real anguish. By evening, she had abandoned her earlier role. A desire to live and blossom at last, like a flower long deprived of air and sunlight, overwhelmed her. It consumed her and led Laurence in turn to indulge in the greatest pleasure she knew, of pouring out her soul in complete trust and candor. Laurence loved her art, not only for its own sake, but also for the freedom and ennoblement of mind and action it brought her. She felt honored by her distinguished connections; she also experienced more passionate affections and, although she was too scrupulous to mention these to Pauline, the still throbbing memories added both charm and intensity to her natural eloquence.

Pauline devoured her friend's words; they fell on her heart like a shower of fire. Pale, hair disheveled, eyes blazing, reclining on her virginal couch, she was as beautiful as an antique nymph in the pale light of the lamp that burned between the two beds. Laurence was struck by her expression. She was afraid she had said too much, and blamed herself, even though her words had been as pure as a mother's to her daughter. Then, forgetting what they had just said to each other, her thoughts turned involuntarily to the theatre as she cried:

"My goodness, how pretty you are, my dear child! Our authors who wrote *Phèdre* hadn't seen you like this. Your pose right now fits perfectly with the modern school; you look exactly like Phèdre . . . not Racine's Phèdre perhaps, but Euripides', when she laments: 'O Gods! Why am I not seated in the shadow of the forest! . . .' If I'm not quoting the Greek," she added with a slight yawn, "it's because I don't know Greek . . . you, on the other hand, probably do . . ."

"Greek? You must be joking!" replied Pauline with a half smile. "What would I use it for?"

"Well, if I had as much time to study as you do, I would want to learn everything!"

There was a moment of silence. Pauline reflected painfully on her life; she wondered what was the use, indeed, of all those marvelous embroideries that had filled her long hours of silence and solitude and had occupied neither her mind nor her heart. She was suddenly appalled at the thought of so many good years wasted, and she realized that she had made a stupid, worthless use of her noblest faculties and her most precious time. She raised herself on her elbow and asked Laurence:

"Why did you compare me to Phèdre? Don't you know that she's a wicked figure? How can you turn vice and crime into something beautiful? . . ."

Laurence did not answer. Exhausted from the previous night's insomnia and at peace with herself as one who, in spite of occasional storms, has found true meaning and goals for her life, she had fallen asleep at the end of her sentence. This prompt and peaceful slumber increased Pauline's anguish and bitterness.

"She's happy," she thought, "happy and satisfied with herself, without effort, without struggle, without doubts . . . and I! . . . How unfair! How terribly unfair!"

Pauline did not sleep a wink that night. The next day, Laurence awoke as easily as she had fallen asleep, and appeared rested and fresh for the day. Her chambermaid arrived with a pretty white dress that she used as a dressing-gown. Laurence rehearsed the role that she was to perform in Lyon in three days' time while the maid combed and braided her magnificent black hair. It was her turn to look beautiful with her disheveled tresses and tragic expression. From time to time, she would elude the chambermaid's hands and pace up and down the apartment, lamenting:

"That's not it! I want my expression to match my feelings!"

She practiced exclamations and bits of dramatic dialogue; she struck various poses in front of Pauline's mirror. The provincial girl was astonished both at the chambermaid's composure in the midst of this behavior, and at Laurence's apparent obliviousness to the world around her. Pauline didn't know whether to laugh at or fear these dramatic outbursts. She was also struck by Laurence's tragic beauty, as Laurence had been struck by hers a few hours earlier. But she said to herself:

"She does all this without passion, with calculated impetuousness and studied grief. Underneath it all, she is utterly calm, utterly happy and I, who should have God's peace in my heart, end up resembling Phèdre!" These were her thoughts when Laurence suddenly said to her:

"I'm doing everything I can to find the pose you had yesterday evening when you were leaning on your elbow . . . I can't do it! It was magnificent. Oh well, perhaps it's too soon. I'll find it later, through inspiration! Inspiration is always based on reminiscence, you know, Pauline. You don't fix your hair right, my dear; you should braid it instead of wearing it drawn back. Here, Suzette will show you how." And while the chambermaid braided one side, Laurence braided the other, and, in a few minutes, Pauline's hairstyle was so attractive and suited her so well that she cried out in surprise:

"My goodness, what skill! I never do my hair this way for fear of wasting too much time. It takes me twice as long."

"We actresses," replied Laurence, "must make ourselves as attractive as possible as quickly as possible."

"But what use is it to me?" moaned Pauline, letting her elbows fall on the dressing table, and staring at the mirror, devastated.

"There!" cried Laurence. "You look like Phèdre again! Stay like that so I can study you!"

Pauline felt her eyes well up with tears. She didn't want Laurence to notice (Pauline feared that more than anything), so she fled to another room, choking back her bitter sobs. Her soul was full of pain and anger, and she didn't understand why these storms were raging within her.

By evening, Laurence was gone. Pauline had wept as she watched her climb into the carriage, this time with regret. For thirty-six hours, Laurence had made her feel really alive, and the thought of the next day terrified her. Exhausted, she fell into bed and fell asleep, heartbroken, hoping never to wake up again. When she did awake, she cast a dejected and fearful look about the room where no trace could be found of the dream Laurence had evoked. She rose slowly, sat mechanically in front of her mirror and tried to braid her hair the way it had been the day before. Suddenly, called back to reality by the song of her canary waking up in its cage, forever happy and indifferent to its captivity, Pauline got up, opened the cage, then the window, and thrust out the sedentary bird, who had no desire to fly away.

"You don't deserve to be free!" she cried as she watched him fly back inside at once.

She returned to her dressing table, untied her braids in a rage, and buried her face in her hands. She stayed that way until her mother awoke. The window was still open, but Pauline did not feel the cold. The canary had returned to its cage and was singing with all its might.

✦ III ✦

A year had passed since Laurence had visited Saint
Front, and people were still talking about the
memorable evening when the famous actress had re-
appeared with such glamour among her fellow coun-
trymen. It would be a serious mistake to assume that
provincial prejudices are difficult to overcome. Whatever people say about this, one can easily win or lose
their goodwill by one's presence and behavior. Some
say that time is a great healer: in the provinces, it is
boredom which brings about change and its justifica-
tion. Any kind of change in the routine of a small town
appears awful at first; but after a while people recognize that it wasn't so terrible, and that, indeed, a thousand curious but timid souls were just waiting for an
example to be set, to launch themselves into a career
of innovation. I know, for example, about a county seat
where the first woman who dared to gallop on horse-
back with an English saddle was shunned as a Cossack
in skirts, and yet the following year, every local lady

requested riding equipment fit for an Amazon, riding-whip included.

Laurence had hardly left when a prompt transformation occurred in everyone's mind. They all wanted to justify their eagerness to meet her by exaggerating her theatrical reputation, or by gradually admitting her fine personal qualities. People vied for the distinction of having spoken to her first, and those who had not been able to bring themselves to visit her claimed that they had strongly encouraged others to do so. That very year, coach service was established between Saint-Front and Mont-Laurens, and several of the town's leading citizens at last ventured a trip to Paris. These are the people who have fifteen thousand francs a year from their land, and who do not travel easily, because they fear that in their absence, chaos will ensue. They all came back full of tales of Laurence's glory and of having told those seated next to them, as the theatre exploded with applause:

"My dear sir, this extraordinary actress used to live in my hometown. She was my wife's closest friend. She had dinner *with us* nearly every evening. We all recognized her talent! I can assure you that when she recited poetry, we all said: 'This young woman will go far!'"

And when the same people returned to Saint-Front, they reported proudly that they had paid their respects to the great actress, had dined at her table, and had spent the evening in her magnificent drawing room ". . . Ah!

What a salon! What furniture! What paintings! And what an entertaining and respectable entourage! Artists, politicians; Monsieur So-and-So, the portrait painter; Madame So-and-So, the soprano; and there was sherbet, and music . . ." and so forth. These wonderful stories made people's heads spin, and everyone exclaimed:

"I always knew that she would succeed! But no one else ever guessed."

All this foolishness had one serious result: it upset poor Pauline, and turned her weariness into despondency. It is impossible to tell whether a few more weeks would have lowered her spirits to the point of complete neglect of her mother, because the old woman suddenly fell gravely ill, so Pauline was quickly recalled to her duty. She recovered her moral and physical strength, and cared for the wretched blind woman with admirable devotion. But her love and zeal could not save the old woman. Madame D— expired in her daughter's arms about fifteen months after Laurence's visit to Saint-Front.

Since their reunion, the two friends had corresponded faithfully. In the midst of her active, bustling life, Laurence liked to think of Pauline. In her mind, she would enter the dark, peaceful house, seek solace next to the geranium-filled window from the noisy crowd around the blind woman's chair. Meanwhile, Pauline was frightened by the monotony of her life and felt an invincible need to shake off the slow death that was engulfing her. In her dreams, she was swept into the whirlwind that surrounded Laurence. The tone of moral superiority that the young provincial girl had first adopted in her letters to the actress, gradually gave way to a painful resignation, which deeply touched her friend. At last, when Pauline expressed heartfelt discontent, Laurence realized, to her dismay, that the exercise of certain virtues, instead of fortifying women's souls, paralyzes them.

"Who, then, can be happy?" she asked her mother one night as she dropped a tear-stained letter on her desk. "How can one find any peace of mind? She who felt so sorry for me at first, for my bohemian life, today complains bitterly about her confinement, and paints such a horrible picture of boredom and solitude, that I am tempted to consider myself happy by comparison, despite the burden of my work and my emotions."

When Laurence heard about the blind woman's death, she consulted her mother, a sensible and deeply caring woman, who had remained her daughter's best friend. The mother tried to dissuade Laurence from her plans to take charge of Pauline's life by inviting her friend to join them as soon as she could.

"But what will become of the poor child now?" Laurence asked. "She has fulfilled her duty to her mother. No other sacred commitment will appear to ennoble her life. An odious existence in a small town is not for her. She feels things deeply and wants to develop her intelligence. Let her come join us; since she wants to discover life, let her do so."

"Yes, she will discover life by observing it," Madame S— replied. "She will see the marvels of art, but her soul will only become more eager and uneasy as a result."

"And yet," the actress continued, "can't you live by observing, and, in understanding what you see, live intelligently? And isn't that what Pauline thirsts for?"

"That's what she says," Madame S— replied, "but she's deceiving you and herself. It's with her heart that she wants to live, the poor child!"

"In that case," Laurence cried out, "can't her heart be nourished by my affection for her? Who in that little town could love her as much as I do? And, if friendship isn't enough, don't you think she could find a man worthy of her love here among us?"

The good Madame S— shook her head.

" She won't want to be loved the way an artist is," she said with a melancholy smile that her daughter understood.

They resumed their conversation the next day. A new letter from Pauline announced that her mother's meager fortune would be eaten away by old debts that her father had left behind and that she was determined to pay immediately. The creditors had been patient with the elderly and infirm Madame D—; but her young, able-bodied daughter couldn't expect the same consideration. They could, without shame, take away her small inheritance. Pauline would await neither threat nor pity: she renounced her parents' inheritance and planned to open a small embroidery shop.

This news eased Laurence's qualms and silenced her mother's objections. Together they went by coach to fetch Pauline and returned to Paris a week later.

It was not without hesitation that Laurence had offered to take in her friend and care for her. She fully expected to find in Pauline some vestige of prejudice and piety. But the truth is that Pauline was not truly devout. She was a proud soul jealous of her own dignity. She found in Catholicism the meaning that suited her character, for all possible meanings can be found in ancient religion: so many centuries have modified it, so many men have had a hand in it, so much intelligence, passion and virtue have brought to it their treasured ideals, their mistakes, or their insights, that finally a thousand doctrines can be found in one, and a thousand different natures can draw from it the excuse or the incentive they need. That is how religion rises and how it falls to ruin.

Pauline was not endowed with the sweet, loving, humble instincts that characterize truly angelic natures. She lacked self-abnegation, so that she always felt unhappy and victimized by her duty. She needed her self-esteem, and the esteem of others, much more than she needed God's love or her fellow man's happiness. While Laurence, less strong and proud, could find consolation for any deprivation and sacrifice in her mother's smile, Pauline, in spite of herself, resented her own mother in the depths of her heart, for having received years of comfort at her daughter's expense. Therefore, it wasn't a feeling of religious austerity that made her hesitate to accept Laurence's offer, it was the fear of not being granted a dignified enough position in Laurence's house.[1]

At first, Laurence misunderstood, thinking that it was the fear of being criticized by bigots that held Pauline back. But that was not what motivated Pauline. Around her, opinions had changed. The great actress's friendship was no longer something to be ashamed of; it had become an honor. There was now a sort of glory in claiming Laurence's interest and friendship. Her latest visit to Saint-Front had been a much greater triumph than her first. She now had to shield herself from the tiresome respects that everyone wished to pay her, and the exclusive preference she showed for Pauline made a thousand people jealous, which flattered Pauline.

After a few hours' discussion, Laurence saw that some scruple still prevented Pauline from accepting her kind offer. Laurence didn't understand this excessive touchiness that couldn't bear the burden of gratitude; but she respected it and reduced herself to tears and prayers in her efforts to overcome the prickly pride of the poor, which the arrogance of some protectors may justify. Should Pauline fear this kind of arrogance from Laurence? Pauline didn't think so; but she couldn't help hesitating a little, and although Laurence was slightly hurt by her mistrust, she made every effort to win her over and thought she would eventually succeed. She triumphed, at least momentarily, thanks to the natural eloquence of her heart; and Pauline, swept along by emotion and curiosity, put a trembling foot on the threshold of her new life, promising herself that she would step back again at the first disappointment she encountered.

The first weeks that Pauline spent in Paris were delightfully quiet. Laurence had been gravely ill and had been given, two months earlier, some time off, which she was devoting to conscientious study. She and her mother were sharing a small, attractive townhouse, surrounded by gardens, where the noise of the city could hardly be heard, and where she received few guests. It was the season when everyone is in the country; theatres are closed, and real artists spend their days quietly meditating. This simple, pretty house, decorated in perfect taste, offered elegant occupations, a peaceful and intelligent life that Laurence had managed to create within a world of intrigue and corruption. It allayed all the fears that Pauline had harbored for many years about her friend. It is true that Laurence had not always been so prudent, surrounded by such company, or so securely established in her own life. She had gained experience and judgment at her own expense, and even though she was still quite young, she had been deeply hurt by ingratitude and wickedness. After suffering a great deal, weeping for her illusions, and keenly regretting the courageous impulses of her youth, she had resigned herself to living life as she found it. She neither feared nor in any way provoked public opinion, and she often sacrificed the headiness of dreams for the sweetness of good behavior; injustice made her angry, but she did not hold any grudges. In a word, she was beginning to resolve, in the exercise of her art as in her private life, a difficult problem. She had grown calm without growing cold; she had contained herself without losing her identity.

Her mother, whose wisdom had sometimes irritated her, but whose kindness always persuaded her, had proved providential. She had not been strong enough to shield Laurence from some mistakes, but had been wise enough to rescue her in time. Laurence had occasionally gone astray, but she never ruined her reputation. Madame S— had sacrificed her principles when necessary, and, whatever anyone says or thinks, that is the most sublime sacrifice motherly love can make. Shame on the mother who abandons her daughter for fear of being considered an accomplice! Madame S— had not been spared this horrible accusation. Laurence in her good-heartedness had understood that her mother had saved her, had snatched her from the delirium that had brought her so close to the abyss. Afterwards, she would have sacrificed everything, a burning passion, a legitimate hope, rather than expose her mother to any new embarassment or insult.

What transpired in the souls of these two women was so delicate, so exquisite, and so mysterious, that Pauline, who was as inexperienced at twenty-five as any fifteen-year-old girl, could in no way understand it. At first, she didn't try to understand; she was simply struck by the happiness and perfect harmony that reigned in this family: the mother, the artistic daughter and the two younger sisters—her pupils, her daughters in a sense, since Laurence guaranteed their well-being through the sweat of her brow and devoted her precious hours of freedom to their education. Their intimacy, their playfulness with one another, was in sharp contrast to the fear and hatred that had cemented the reciprocal attachment of Pauline and her mother. Pauline made this painful observation without remorse (hadn't she overcome the temptation to abandon her duties a thousand times?) but with something resembling shame. How could she not feel humiliated when she found more devotion and true domestic virtue in the elegant home of an actress, than she had been able to practice within her own austere household. How many burning thoughts had made her blush as she lay awake alone at night, in the lamplight of her chaste cell! And now she saw Laurence, lying on a sultan's sofa in her actress's boudoir, reading Shakespeare's poetry aloud to her enraptured younger sisters while their mother, still cheerful, sprightly and tastefully dressed, prepared their clothes for the following day, occasionally casting a blissful look at this handsome group, so dear to her heart. In this scene were gathered artistic enthusiasm, kindness, poetry, affection and wisdom, and above all a sense of moral beauty, self-respect and courage. It seemed like a dream to Pauline, and she refused to believe what she saw. Perhaps her reluctance was rooted in the fear of finding herself inferior to Laurence.

In spite of these doubts and this secret anguish, Pauline responded admirably at first to her new existence. Forever proud in spite of her poverty, she managed to make herself genuinely useful, so that she would not be a financial drain. With extraordinary stoicism for a young provincial girl, she refused the pretty dresses that Laurence offered her. She kept to her plain mourning clothes, her little black dress with its dainty white collar, and her simple, unadorned hairstyle. She willingly helped with the management of the household, which Laurence could only supervise from afar, and daily chores which were becoming harder for Madame S—. Pauline managed to economize without diminishing elegance or comfort. Moreover, by resuming her needlework, she created pretty embroideries for the two little girls' dresses. She also became their tutor and governess between Laurence's lessons. She helped Laurence learn new roles by listening to her practice. In short, she managed to create a humble yet significant place for herself within the family, and her pride was satisfied with the respect and affection that she received in return.

This carefree life continued until early winter. Every day, Laurence invited two or three longtime friends to dinner; and after supper, six to eight intimate acquaintances would come for tea in her drawing room and discuss art, literature, even a little politics and social philosophy. These conversations, full of charm and interest for distinguished minds, resembled in taste, wit and politeness those that had taken place during the last century at Mademoiselle de Verrière's house,[2] on the corner of the rue and boulevard Caumartin. But these discussions were more animated: the spirit of our times is deeper, and serious questions can be bandied about, even between the sexes, without ridicule or pedantry. The particular intelligence of women may consist for some time yet in knowing how to ask questions and how to listen; but they are already allowed to understand what they hear and to expect serious answers to their questions.

As chance would have it, throughout that late fall, Laurence's intimate circle consisted exclusively of women or men of a certain age, without amorous pretensions. Let's say in passing that it was not only chance that dictated that choice, but Laurence's increasingly marked taste for serious matters and serious people. Around a remarkable woman, everything tends to become harmonious and to take on the hue of her thoughts and feelings. Therefore, Pauline did not have a single opportunity to see anyone who might have disturbed her peace of mind; and what was strange, even in her own eyes, was that she was already beginning to find this life monotonous, this society a little pale, and to wonder whether the image that she had constructed of Laurence's whirlwind existence did not need a bit more thrilling reality. She was surprised to fall back into the same despondency that she had fought against for so long in her solitude. And, in order to justify this strange disquietude, she convinced herself that in her isolation she had developed a tendency towards depression that nothing could cure.

But this situation did not last. However reluctant the actress was to re-enter the whirl of society, however careful she was to shy away from frivolity or dangerous liaisons in her intimate circle, winter arrived. The châteaux lost their guests to the Parisian salons, the theaters revived their repertoires, the public called back its favorite actors. Commotion, hasty work, worries and the desire for success invaded Laurence's quiet household. Other men besides old friends were allowed to cross the threshold and enter the sanctuary. Men of letters came, and acquaintances from the theater, as well as officials in charge of funding the dramatic arts. Some were notable because of their talent, others because of their beauty and elegance, and still others because of their influence and money. They trickled in one by one at first, then by throngs, and animated the blank screen where Pauline had burnt to see the world of her dreams appear at last before her eyes. Laurence, who was used to this parade of celebrities, was unmoved. However, her life had to change course; her schedule became busier, her mind more occupied with study, her artistic sensibilities more stimulated by contact with the public. Her mother and sisters followed her peacefully, like faithful satellites in her dazzling trajectory. But Pauline! . . . Here at last her soul began to blossom and, within her soul, the drama of her life began to unfold.

⋆ IV ⋆

Among Laurence's young admirers, there was a certain Montgenays, who dabbled at writing prose and poetry, but who, from modesty or disdain, did not claim to be a man of letters. He was witty, worldly, well-educated, and somewhat talented. The son of a banker, he had inherited a considerable fortune and did not attempt to increase it. Instead, he could think of no nobler use for it than buying horses, having a private box at several theatres, a fine table at home, beautiful furniture, a collection of paintings, and sizeable debts. Although he was blessed with neither a great mind nor a great heart, it should be said in his defense that he was less frivolous and ignorant than most of the rich young men of today. He had no principles, but on grounds of expediency detested scandals; he was fairly corrupt, but his manners, however profligate, were elegant; he was capable of harming others on occasion, but would not do it on purpose; he was skeptical by education, habit, and breeding, and given to the vices of the world because he lacked principles and good examples, rather than by nature or by choice. Furthermore, he was an intelligent critic, a decent writer, a pleasant conversationalist, a connoisseur and dilettante in every art form, a tasteful patron, who knew about and dabbled at a little of everything; he frequented the best circles without ostentation and consorted with the worst without impudence; he spent most of his fortune, not by helping artists in need, but by lavishly hosting celebrities. He was welcome everywhere and fit in perfectly wherever he went. He was considered a great man by the ignorant, and an enlightened man by ordinary folk. Intellectuals valued his conversation in comparison to that of other men in society, and snobs tolerated him because he knew how to flatter them while poking fun at them. In short, this Montgenays was precisely what society calls a wit, or what artists call a man of taste. Poor, he would have been lost in a crowd of ordinary men, but because of his wealth, people were grateful that he was not a Jew, a fool, or a madman.

He was one of those people you meet everywhere, whom everyone knows at least by sight, and who knows everyone by name. There was no circle where he wasn't admitted, no theatre where he didn't have entry backstage, no company where he didn't have stock, no administration where he didn't have influence, no circle where he wasn't a founding member or sponsor. Dandyism hadn't been his key to conquering the world; he had a dispassionate expertise, full of egotism, was somewhat conceited, and had enough wit to appear more generous, more intelligent and more artistic than he really was.

His position had for some time put him in contact with Laurence, but their acquaintance had at first been remote, purely conventional; and if Montgenays had occasionally been gallant, it had always been within acceptable boundaries. Laurence had mistrusted him a little at first, being quite aware that there is no more dangerous company for the reputation of a young actress than a gentleman of this sort. But when she saw that Montgenays wasn't courting her, that he visited her often enough to make some claims and yet did not make any, she was thankful for his respectful behavior; and not wishing to appear prudish or a coquette by being coy, she let him enter her inner circle of friends, received without hesitation a thousand small favors from him, which he rushed to offer respectfully, and did not hesitate to count him among her true friends and to admire him for being handsome, young, influential and modest.

Montgenay's outward behavior justified her trust. Oddly enough, however, he resented this trust even while he felt flattered by it. When people believed he was Laurence's friend or lover, his vanity was gratified. But when he thought that in reality she treated him like a man of little consequence, he was secretly offended and pondered how to take his revenge someday.

The truth is that he was not in love with her. For the past three years at least, while he had been on increasingly intimate terms with her, his heart had remained calm and untouched. He was one of those men, jaded by secret corruption, who can only feel strong desires when their vanity is at stake. When he had met Laurence, her reputation and talent were growing; but neither was well enough established for him to attach a great price to her conquest. Besides, he was cunning enough to know that his place in society could not ensure that he would succeed. He could see that Laurence was too dignified to be duped by anything but love. Furthermore, he knew that even though she would overlook public opinion when moved by generosity, she still rejected the idea of being protected and helped by a lover. He inquired about her past, her intimate life: he discovered that any gift except flowers would be rejected as a deep insult, and, while these discoveries increased his respect for Laurence, they encouraged him to conquer her pride, because it would be a difficult conquest that would add to his reputation. That is precisely why he had skillfully penetrated her inner circle, thinking that the first step was to remove any misgivings about his intentions.

Three years had passed, and the opportunity to make a move had not presented itself. Laurence's talent had become undeniable, her fame had increased, she was financially secure, and, moreover, she had not fallen in love. She lived coiled upon herself, firm, calm, occasionally sad, but resolved not to risk a stormy relationship. Perhaps, after years of reflection, she had become more discriminating and couldn't find a man worthy of her choice. . . . Montgenays anxiously wondered whether she was contemptuous or courageous. Some people thought that she was secretly in love with him and asked him why he seemed so indifferent to her. Too clever to allow them to see through him, Montgenays answered that he had too much respect for her to think of being anything but a friend and brother to Laurence. These words were reported to Laurence, and she was asked whether her pride would ever allow her to encourage poor Montgenays to declare his true feelings for her.

"I think he's shy," she replied, "but not so shy that he would not know how to declare his love, if he ever happens to fall in love."

When this reply reached Montgenays, he didn't know whether it signified ironic resentment or quiet indifference. At times, his vanity was so piqued that he was ready to try anything to find out, but the fear of losing everything held him back, and time passed without his being able to escape the vicious circle which each week carried him from hope to despondency and made him hover between hypocrisy and insolence. He was never able to find the right time for a declaration that would not appear foolish, or a retreat that would not seem ridiculous. Above all, he was afraid of making a fool of himself. Pauline's entry upon the scene he saw as a boon; this inexperienced girl's beauty gave him the idea for a new plan that would not change his original objective.

He devised the sort of simple plot that usually works, because so many women have a tendency to foolish vanity. He thought that if he feigned a slight inclination for Pauline, he would awaken in Laurence the desire to compete with her friend. After an absence of several months from Paris, he made his entrance into Laurence's salon one evening when Pauline, surprised to see so many new faces joining the usual circle by the hour, was beginning to be conscious of her dowdy black dress and stiff collar. In this circle, she noticed several actresses, all pretty or at least cleverly seductive; when she compared herself to them, or to Laurence, she rightly concluded that her own features were more symmetrical, more classic and that a few elegant garments would make that obvious to every eye.

While she moved about in the salon to make tea, check the lamps and attend, as was her custom, to the small tasks that she had voluntarily taken on, she glanced sadly at the mirror and was irritated by the sight of her little nun's costume. It was precisely then, in the mirror, that she met Montgenays' eyes, which were fastened upon her every move. She had not heard his name announced; she had not noticed him in the foyer when he had arrived. He was the first really elegant and attractive man whom she had ever met. She was struck by a kind of terror; she looked at herself anxiously, and found her dress shabby, her hands red, her shoes heavy, her gait awkward. She wished to escape from his eyes, which followed her everywhere, observed her confusion, and seemed to understand immediately what she was feeling. A few moments later, she noticed that Montgenays was talking about her to Laurence; for they whispered to each other, looking at her.

"Is what I see here a lady's maid or a lady's companion?" Montgenays asked, although he knew Pauline's story perfectly well.

"Neither," Laurence replied. "She's my friend from the provinces whom I often told you about. What do you think of her?"

Montgenays first affected not to answer, keeping his eyes on Pauline; then he told Laurence, in an odd tone that she had not heard before—since he had saved it to impress her at the right moment:

"Admirably beautiful, deliciously pretty!"

"Indeed!" cried Laurence, very surprised by this. "You make me very happy by telling me this! Come, I will introduce you."

Without waiting for his answer, she seized his arm and led him to the other side of the salon, where Pauline tried to compose herself by putting away her embroidery loom.

"My dear child, let me introduce you to a friend you don't know yet, but who has looked forward to meeting you," Laurence said.

Then, after having named Montgenays to Pauline, who was too confused to hear anything, Laurence went to greet a friend who had just arrived; and, changing groups, she left Montgenays and Pauline face to face, practically by themselves, in a corner of the salon.

Pauline had never yet spoken to a man so well-coiffed, so perfumed, with such a perfect tie and shoes. You cannot imagine what an impression these elegant trifles make on the imagination of a provincial girl. A white hand, a diamond pinned on a shirt, a varnished shoe, a corsage: these are refinements which are noticed in a salon only in their absence. But when a traveling salesman exhibits these outrageous attributes in a small town, every eye is glued on him. I don't wish to imply that all hearts will be his, but he will be quite a fool if he doesn't catch a few.

Had Pauline possessed greater intelligence and self-respect, she would soon have shaken off this provincial reaction; but she could not help finding Montgenays' remarks both charming and well-bred. She had blushed at the idea of being moved simply by a man's appearance. But her first impression was confirmed when she found that his mind was as elegant as his whole person. In addition, the special attention he was paying her, his obvious desire to be introduced to her, hidden as she was in a corner among china cups and flower vases, the timid pleasure he seemed to take in asking her about her tastes, her impressions and her friendships, treating her like an enlightened being, capable of understanding and judging everything, roused her from her usual apathy. Pauline was unaware of the affectation, triteness and dishonesty of worldly manners. She apologized for her great ignorance; Montgenays pretended to admire her modesty and regret her lack of self-confidence. Pauline gradually ventured to demonstrate her wit, good taste and fine intellect. The fact is that she was extraordinarily gifted, considering her past cloistered life, but among artists used to dazzling conversations, she would occasionally fall into platitudes. Although her mind was naturally distinguished, which preserved her from triviality, one could easily see that she had not fully matured. A better man than Montgenays would have wanted to participate in her development; but this vain creature secretly conceived contempt for Pauline's intelligence and decided immediately that he would use her as a toy, a tool—if necessary, a victim.

Who could have guessed that such an apparently detached and languid man could make so sharp and cruel a decision? No one, certainly. Laurence, despite all her sophistication, could not guess, and Pauline less than anyone.

When Laurence returned, remembering with solicitude that she had left Pauline unsure and embarrassed with Montgenays, she was stunned to find her sparkling, playful, glowing with a new beauty, and almost as comfortable as if she had spent her entire life in society.

"Look at your provincial friend," whispered an old actor of her acquaintance; "isn't it marvelous how a girl can acquire cleverness all of a sudden?"

Laurence paid little attention to this joke. And the next day, she was not aware that Montgenays had come to visit an hour early, knowing that Laurence would not return from her rehearsal till four o'clock. Between the time of his arrival and four o'clock, he had waited in the drawing room, not alone, but hovering over Pauline's loom.

In bright daylight, Pauline had found him terribly old. Even though he was merely thirty, excesses had already marked his face, and in the provinces, the concept of beauty is always bound to wholesomeness and health. To her credit, Pauline did not yet understand that debauchery marks people's faces with a certain grandeur and poetry. How many men of our romantic era have been considered thinkers and poets, just because they have bags under their eyes and prematurely wrinkled foreheads! How many were taken for geniuses when they were merely ill!

But the charm of his conversation entranced Pauline even more than it had on the previous day. All the insinuating flattery, which any worldly woman will recognize for what it is, fell on the poor recluse's dry and barren soul like salutary rain. Her mind, having been deprived of legitimate pleasures for so long, was blossoming under the treacherous breath of seduction, and what deplorable seduction! It came from a perfectly cold man, who despised her credulity and wanted to use her to conquer Laurence.

· V ·

The first person to notice Pauline's foolish infatuation was Madame S—. With keen maternal insight, she had divined Montgenays' scheme and tactics. She had never been duped by his feigned indifference and had always mistrusted him, which in turn made Montgenays declare that Madame S— was, like all artists' mothers, a narrow-minded, sullen woman, set against her daughter's success. As he courted Pauline, Madame S— (in her solicitude for her daughter) feared that his ruse would succeed, and that Laurence would feel slighted because she had not been noticed by a fashionable man. She should have known Laurence better; but Madame S—, in spite of her genuinely high intelligence, was sometimes as fearful as a young mother who sees danger at every turn. So she was afraid that Laurence would discover Montgenays' budding love affair, and, instead of calling upon her daughter's reason and affection to rescue Pauline, she tried to open Pauline's eyes and point out her imprudence.

However, even though she proceeded with kindness and delicacy, her words were not well received. Pauline was giddy with love; She would rather have had her life snatched away than give up the belief that she was adored. Madame S— was angered by Pauline's brusque rejection of her warnings. They exchanged words, the one implying Pauline's inferiority, the other tinged with pride at her triumph over Laurence. Frightened by what she had let slip, Pauline told Montgenays, who assumed with delight that the mother was echoing her daughter's vexation. He believed that he was achieving his goal, and like a gambler doubling his stakes, became twice as attentive to Pauline. He had already lied shamelessly to her about a love he did not feel. She had pretended not to believe him; but the poor soul believed him only too well! Even though she struggled with all her might, Montgenays was nonetheless sure of reaching her very soul. He scorned the final step in his victory and waited for Laurence's reaction to decide whether to conquer Pauline or to drop her.

Laurence, who was absorbed by her studies and forced to spend most of her days at the theatre with morning rehearsals and evening performances, had not noticed the progress Montgenays was making with Pauline. She was struck by Pauline's reaction one evening, when a witty elderly actor named Lavallée, who had been Laurence's mentor since her debut, passed harsh judgement on Montgenays' mind and character. He declared him more vulgar than any vulgar man; and when Laurence defended at least his sentimental qualities, Lavallée exclaimed:

"I know you will all disagree with me, because everyone likes him. Do you know why they like him? It's because he is not evil."

"It seems to me that that's something," Pauline shot back with a bitter, meaningful glance at the old artist, who was the best of men.

"It's less than nothing," he replied, "because he isn't good, and that's why I don't like him, if you must know. You can't hope for anything and must fear everything from a man who is neither good nor bad."

Several voices were raised in defense of Montgenays; Laurence's being perhaps the loudest; yet she couldn't excuse him when Lavallée pointed out that he did not have a single real friend, and that no one had ever seen him righteously indignant, which is the sign of a great and generous heart. At that point, Pauline could no longer control herself: Laurence, she said, deserved Lavallée's criticism more than anyone for letting him attack one of her closest and most devoted friends without showing resentment or rage. During this strange outburst, Pauline was trembling and broke her tapestry needle. Her agitation was so extreme that the salon fell silent and all eyes turned to her in surprise. She understood her blunder and tried to repair it by offering a general criticism of people's behavior in these sorts of cases.

"It saddens me to see how indifferently people can listen to someone tear someone else apart and then, moments later, greet that maligned person and shake his hand without blushing," she cried. "I may be just an ignorant girl from the provinces, but I can't get used to it. . . . You, Monsieur Lavallée, should agree with me since I'm having an outburst of the righteous anger you criticize Monsieur Montgenays for lacking."

As she finished speaking, Pauline tried to smile at Laurence, to soften the impact of her words. She managed to fool everyone except her astute friend, who noticed a tear in the corner of her eye.

Lavallée agreed with Pauline and, with extraordinary talent, began to act out a scene from Molière's *Misanthrope* dealing with human friendship. He played this role in the tradition of Fleury,[3] and was so taken with the character of Alceste that he had, unwittingly, come to identify more closely with him than his own nature might have dictated. Artists are thus often drawn by instinct halfway to a character that they reproduce with deep affection, and their success at this creation completes the total merging; that's how art, which expresses our internal life, often becomes life itself for us.

When Laurence was once more alone with her friend that evening, she questioned her with a trust born of true affection. The fear and reserve that marked her friend's answers surprised her, and then began to worry her.

"Listen, my darling," she said as she left her, "all the trouble you're taking to prove to me that you don't love him only makes me more afraid that you really do. I can't say that it saddens me, because I think he's worthy of your esteem; but I don't know whether he's in love with you, and I'd like to be sure. If he is, it seems to me that he should have said something to me before announcing himself to you. I am your mother now! My knowledge of the world and its dangers gives me the right, the duty, to guide and enlighten you if necessary. I beg you, don't listen to the seductive words of any man without consulting me. Let me first look into the heart that offers itself to you; for I can be objective, and I don't think anyone could fool me when it comes to Pauline, the person I love most in the world after my mother and sisters."

These tender words wounded Pauline to the very depths of her soul. She felt that Laurence wanted to dominate her by assuming the right to guide her. Pauline couldn't forget that Laurence had once appeared to her to be a lost and depraved soul. Her proud prayers, like the Pharisees', had risen towards God, begging a bit of mercy for this outcast soul, denied entrance at the temple door. Laurence had spoiled Pauline, as one spoils a child, with excessive tenderness and devotion. In her letters, she had repeated too often that Pauline was for her like an angel of pure light, whose celestial presence protected Laurence from every evil thought. Pauline had grown accustomed to posing as a madonna for Laurence; to receive a maternal admonition from her at this point seemed outrageous. She was so angry and humiliated that she could not sleep. By the next day, she had overcome her unfair reaction, and thanked her friend heartily for her kind concern; however, she still could not bring herself to admit her feelings for Montgenays.

Once awakened, Laurence's suspicion did not go away. She had a talk with her mother, reproaching her a little for not having mentioned her own suspicions earlier, and, respecting Pauline's reluctance, which she attributed to excessive modesty, she began to observe Montgenays' every step. It didn't take her long to confirm that Madame S— had guessed correctly, and, three days later, she had the proof she was looking for. She caught Pauline and Montgenays engaged in an animated tête-à-tête, pretended not to see Pauline's agitation, and, that very evening, summoned Montgenays to her study where she told him:

"I thought you were my friend, and yet I have to reproach you for a serious breach of trust, Montgenays. You're in love with Pauline, but you have not confided in me. You're courting her without having asked my permission."

She uttered these words with some emotion, because she really blamed Montgenays in her heart, and his strange behavior made her fear the worst for Pauline. Montgenays wanted to attribute her reproachful tone to her own feelings for him. He put on an impenetrable expression, and decided to remain on the defensive until Laurence expressed the jealousy he assumed she felt. He denied his love for Pauline, but with intentional clumsiness so as to worry Laurence even more.

His lack of frankness did alarm her, but only because of her friend. She hadn't the slightest intention of becoming personally involved in this affair.

Montgenays, in spite of his sophistication, was foolish enough to be mistaken; and, when he thought that he had at last roused Laurence's jealousy and anger, he risked a dramatic twist that he had long contemplated. He confessed that his love for Pauline was only a self-delusion, a hopeless effort, useless probably, to numb a deep sorrow, to overcome an unfortunate passion. . . . A devastating look from Laurence stopped him just as he was about to betray himself and save Pauline. He realized that the right moment had not yet come, and held his dramatic declaration for a more promising encounter. When pressed by Laurence's stern questions, he turned in a thousand directions, invented a convoluted story, protested that he did not think Pauline loved him, and left without promising to love Pauline in earnest, without consenting to tell her the truth, without reassuring Laurence, and yet without giving her the right to condemn him.

If Montgenays had been clumsy enough to make a mistake, he was clever enough to repair it. He had a tortuous and childish mind which, through a complicated series of twists and turns, cleverly, laboriously, wound its way toward a terrible fiasco. He kept Laurence wondering for several weeks. She had never thought him conceited and could not bring herself to think him a coward. She saw Pauline's passion and pain, but she had such a deep desire for her happiness that she didn't dare to keep Montgenays away in order to save her.

"No, I don't think he was making an impudent insinuation," she told her mother, "when he told me that an unhappy love kept him waffling. I thought for a moment that that was what he meant, but it would be too odious. I believe him to be a man of honor. He has always treated me with kindness and respect. He can't suddenly have decided to toy with me and destroy my friend at the same time. He wouldn't think me simple enough to be his dupe."

"I think he's capable of anything," Madame S— replied. "Ask Lavallée what he thinks; let him know what's happening. He's a man you can trust, he thinks clearly and he is devoted to you."

"I know," said Laurence, "but I can't divulge a secret that Pauline refuses to reveal to me: I can't betray such a delicate mystery, when I've discovered it in spite of her; Pauline would be mortally wounded and, proud as she is, she would never forgive me as long as she lived. Besides, Lavallée has an exaggerated view; he hates Montgenays; he can't judge him fairly. Think how badly we will hurt Pauline if we are wrong! If Montgenays is in love with her (and why not? She's so beautiful, so chaste, so intelligent!), we'd be destroying her future by keeping away a man who might marry her and give her the social rank she surely deserves; you know how she suffers, depending on us for a living. Her situation is more difficult than she admits; she craves independence, and only money can give her that."

"But what if he doesn't marry her!" cried Madame S—. "I, for one, don't think he has any intention to do that."

"And I," retorted Laurence, "can't believe that a man like him could be wicked or crazy enough to think he could have Pauline any other way."

"Well, if you believe that," replied her mother, "try to keep them apart. Close your door to him: then he'll be forced to declare his love. You can be sure that if he truly loves her he'll manage to overcome any obstacle and prove his devotion with an honorable proposal."

"But he might have been telling the truth," Laurence continued, "when he spoke of an unfinished affair which prevents him from declaring his love. Doesn't that happen all the time? A man can hover for years between two women, one who holds him through flirtation, while the other attracts him through her sweetness. There comes a time when the false passion yields to true love, when the man sees his heartless mistress's failure and recognizes the qualities of his generous friend. Today, if we challenge poor Montgenay's hesitation, if we put a knife to his throat and a contract in his hand, he will, if only for spite, abandon Pauline, who may die of grief, and return to the bosom of his treacherous lover, who will finally leave him with a shriveled or broken heart. On the other hand, if we act with patience and caution, and let him see Pauline, he will compare her to the other woman, realize that she's the only one worthy of his love, and end up declaring his preference. What is there to fear from a test like that? That Pauline will not truly love him? She already does. That she may let him take advantage of her? That's impossible. He wouldn't try and she wouldn't let him."

These arguments shook Madame S— a little . . . all she asked of Laurence was to prevent the tête-à-têtes that Pauline's errands and occupations allowed too easily and too frequently between herself and Montgenays. It was agreed that Laurence would take her friend with her to the theatre more often. They thought that Montgenay's passion would grow as it became more difficult to talk to Pauline, while seeing her would increase his admiration.

But it was incredibly difficult to convince Pauline to leave the house. She withdrew from Laurence into a painful silence, so that Laurence was reduced to playing a childish game with her, offering her reasons to go out that she knew her friend did not accept. She argued that Pauline's health was being impaired by the constant housework, that she needed to go out and enjoy herself. She even asked a doctor to prescribe a more active life. Everything failed in the face of Pauline's passive resistance, the strength of a cold, unresponsive temperament. Finally, it occurred to Laurence to ask her friend as a favor to her to help her get dressed and change costumes in her dressing room at the theatre. Her chambermaid was clumsy, she said, Madame S— wasn't feeling well, worn down by the constant bustle, and Laurence herself was overwhelmed. Only her friend's tender care could ease the daily burden of her professional obligations. Pushed to the limit, and prompted, too, by her remaining friendship and devotion, Pauline yielded, but with secret reluctance. Witnessing Laurence's triumphs each day was a source of suffering that she had never overcome; and now, her suffering grew more acute. With a sense of foreboding, Pauline began to foresee her misfortune. Since Montgenays had convinced himself that there was some hope of winning over the actress, he occasionally unwittingly revealed his contempt for the provincial girl. Pauline didn't want to see the truth; she averted her eyes in terror; yet, in spite of herself, sorrow and jealousy had entered her soul.

◆ VI ◆

Montgenays noted the precautions Laurence had taken to keep him away from Pauline; he also noticed the deep sadness that had overcome the young woman. He pressed her with questions. But since she remained on the defensive with him, and would talk to him only in private, he could not be sure of anything. Nevertheless, he saw the authority that, out of genuine friendship for Pauline, Laurence was unafraid to assume over her, and he saw too that Pauline submitted to it with a kind of contained indignation. He thought that Laurence was beginning to make Pauline suffer because she was jealous of her. He could not imagine that his preference for another woman could leave Laurence indifferent and loyal to her friend.

He purposely continued playing this whimsical, deliberately inconsistent role, baffling both women. He would spend weeks without visiting them, then would suddenly become persistent again, wearing a worried, tormented look, pretending to be ill-tempered when he felt calm, and feigning indifference when he surely felt resentful. This moodiness annoyed Laurence and upset Pauline, who was becoming more bitter every day. She wondered why Montgenay, after having pursued her so eagerly, was so casual about overcoming the obstacles that had arisen between them. She secretly resented Laurence for having shattered her illusions, and refused to recognize that in enlightening her, her friend was doing her a favor. When she questioned Montgenays as calmly as she could about his frequent absences, he replied, when they were alone, that he had been occupied with urgent business; but when Laurence was present, he claimed only to have had a vague need to be alone or to amuse himself.

One day, Pauline told him in front of Madame S—, whose constant presence was a torment to her, that he must have some amorous attachment in high society because he frequented their circle of artists so rarely these days. Montgenays answered wryly:

"Even if that were the case, I don't see how someone as serious as yourself could be interested in a young man's foolish behavior."

At that very moment, Laurence came into the drawing room. She saw at once the forced, painful smile on Pauline's face. She was sick at heart. Laurence approached her friend and tenderly put her arm around her shoulders. Pauline, recalled to a feeling of affection for her rival whom she couldn't blame for her current suffering, turned her head gently and touched

Laurence's hand lightly with her lips. She seemed to ask her forgiveness for having despised and defamed her in her heart. Laurence only half understood this gesture, and drew the poor child nearer, in profound sympathy. Then, Pauline, making an effort to swallow her tears, declared with a wry smile:

"I was complaining to *your* friend about the way he's been neglecting you."

Laurence stared at Montgenays. He mistook her severe look for a display of feminine anger, and, drawing closer to her, he asked with an expression that made Pauline shiver:

"And are *you* complaining, Madame?"

"Yes, I am," Laurence replied in a tone even sterner than her look.

"Well, that makes up for my suffering when I'm not with you," said Montgenays, kissing her hand.

Laurence felt Pauline shiver in her arms.

"You suffered?" exclaimed Madame S——, who was trying to probe Montgenay's soul. "That's not what you were saying a moment ago. You were talking about 'a young man's follies'; that should have distracted you somewhat from the pain of separation."

"I was responding to your joke," Montgenays replied. "But I couldn't have fooled Laurence. She knows perfectly well that there can be no more folly or frivolous affection for the man she honors with her esteem."

As he spoke, his eyes shone with a fire that gave his words a meaning that was the complete opposite of calm friendship. Pauline's eyes were fixed upon his every movement: she saw the look he gave Laurence, and it pierced her to the heart. She paled and brusquely pushed Laurence's hand away from her. Laurence was caught by surprise. She looked questioningly at her mother, and her mother signalled to her. A moment later, the two women left, on a pretext, to walk back and forth together in the garden terrace. Laurence was finally beginning to understand the evil mystery in which Pauline's cowardly lover had cloaked himself.

"What I'm beginning to understand," she told her mother emotionally, "upsets and appalls me. I'm so shocked, and don't dare to believe it yet."

"I have been convinced of his plotting for a long time," Madame S— replied. "He's playing an odious role in order to win you, and he's sacrificing Pauline to succeed and satisfy his vanity."

"Well," Laurence added, "I must tell Pauline; but before doing that, I have to be sure; I'll let him make his move, and I'll unmask him once he's caught in the trap. Since he wants to engage me in a trite and vulgar dramatic plot, I will use the same means, and we'll see which of us is the better actor. I can't believe he has the audacity to compete with me when he's not even in the profession."

"Be careful!" cried Madame S—. "He'll become your deadly enemy and a literary enemy at that."

"Since I can't help having enemies in the press," replied Laurence, "why should I worry about one more?

My duty is to protect Pauline, and since I can't bear to have her think that I would betray her, I will forewarn her of my plan."

"That will guarantee its failure," replied Madame S—. "Pauline is more deeply attached to him than you think. She's suffering and is beside herself with love. She doesn't want you to enlighten her. She'll hate you for it."

"Well, let her hate me then," Laurence cried tearfully; "I would rather bear that pain than see her fall victim to such infamy."

"In that case, prepare for the worst; but if you want to succeed, don't warn her. She would tell Montgenays, and you would have compromised yourself for no reason."

Laurence listened to her mother's advice. When she returned to the salon, Pauline and Montgenays had already exchanged a few words that had reassured the wretched dupe. Pauline was beaming; she kissed her friend with a look filled with hatred and with the irony of her triumph. Laurence hid her mortal pain, and now understood clearly the game Montgenays was playing.

Unwilling to stoop to giving the slightest hope to this scoundrel, she copied his manner and tone, cloaking herself in mysterious and bizarre behavior. She sometimes affected the worried melancholy of a misunderstood lover, sometimes the forced happiness of courageous resolution. Then she pretended to fall into desperate despondency again. Unable to exchange provocative glances with Montgenays, she waited for him to look at her when Pauline's back was turned, and then stared at Pauline with a pretense of jealousy. In the end, she succeeded so well in acting like a woman who was in despair, but so proud that she would prefer death to the humiliation of rejection, that Montgenays became enraptured and forgot his own role, seeking instead only to understand hers. His vanity interpreted her behavior to fit his desire; but he still did not dare make his move, because Laurence couldn't bring herself to provoke a straightforward declaration on his part. Even though she was an excellent actress, she was unable to give a convincing portrayal of a character she didn't like. One day she told Lavallée, whom her mother had confided in against her daughter's wishes (he had in fact guessed the whole thing on his own):

"However hard I try, I play this role badly. It's the same as in a bad play, when I can't put myself in the situation. You remember when we were on stage with poor Mélidor, who delivered the most passionate lines with utter calm; we avoided looking at each other for fear of bursting into laughter. Well, with this Montgenays, it's exactly the same. When you're there and my eyes meet yours, I feel like bursting; so, in order to keep my sad countenance, I think of Pauline's misfortune, and that puts me right back into my role but, at my expense, for it makes my heart ache so. Ah! I did not know it was so much harder to act in real life than on stage!"

"I'll help you," Lavallée replied, "because I can see that you'll never be able to unmask him by yourself. Trust me to force him out without compromising you."

One evening, Laurence played Hermione in the tragedy *Andromaque.*[4] The public had been waiting a long time for her debut in this role. Perhaps she had carefully studied the role recently or maybe the sight of the full house energized her more than usual, or she may have needed to invest in this beautiful creation all the energy and artistry she had been employing so unpleasantly with Montgenays for the past two weeks. Whatever the reason, she was magnificent, and received more applause than ever before. It wasn't so much Laurence's genius as her reputation that made her so desirable to Montgenays. On days when she was tired and the public responded less warmly towards her, he slept more peacefully, with the thought that he didn't have to succeed with her. But when she received several curtain calls and people threw bouquets of flowers to her, he couldn't sleep and spent the night plotting her seduction. This particular evening, he was watching the performance from a small box directly above the stage, with Pauline, Madame S— and Lavallée. He was so agitated by the frenzied applause that the beautiful actress received, that he became oblivious to Pauline's presence. Two or three times he bumped her with his elbow (everyone knows how narrow those boxes are) while clapping wildly. He wanted Laurence to see him, to hear him above the roaring crowd; and when Pauline complained bitterly that he was so quick to applaud that she couldn't hear the last words of each speech, he rudely retorted:

"Why do you need to hear, anyway? Can you even understand what's going on?"

There were times when, despite his practiced diplomacy, Montgenays could not repress open contempt for this wretched girl. He didn't love her, in spite of her beauty and her really excellent qualities; and he was secretly indignant at the unsuspecting self-assurance of this young bourgeoise, who actually thought she could outshine the brilliant actress in his eyes. He too was weary, disgusted with his role. Even the evil sometimes find it difficult to relish the harm they do. If not remorse, then shame will occasionally paralyze potential perversity.

Pauline began to feel dizzy. At first, she kept silent but after a moment she said she could no longer bear the heat; she stood up and left the box. The good Madame S—, who felt genuinely sorry for her, followed her and took her to Laurence's dressing room, where Pauline fell onto the sofa and lost consciousness. While Madame S— and Laurence's chambermaid were loosening her corset and trying to revive her, Montgenays, incapable of imagining the harm he had done, was still admiring and applauding the magnificent actress. When the act was over, Lavallée drew him aside, and said, with the most sincere expression any actor ever wore on stage:

"Do you realize that our Laurence has never been more astounding than today? Her eyes, her voice, have taken on a glow that I have never seen before. It worries me."

"Why?" Montgenays replied. "Are you afraid that she might have a fever?"

"Without a doubt; it was feverish energy," Lavallée replied. "I can recognize it; I know that such a delicate, fragile woman can't create such an effect without becoming dangerously excited. I would bet that Laurence will lie exhausted during the whole intermission. That's what happens to women whose strength derives solely from passion."

"Let's go see her!" Montgenays cried out, standing up.

"Absolutely not," Lavallée replied, making him sit down again with a solemnity that made him laugh to himself. "That would hardly help to calm her."

"What do you mean?" Montgenays asked.

"I don't mean anything," the actor replied, with the look of a man who fears he has betrayed himself.

This game lasted the whole intermission. Montgenays was suspicious but couldn't understand the situation. He was too vain to realize that he was being made fun of. Besides, he was dealing with a much stronger opponent, and Lavallée said to himself:

"Yes, sir! You want to take on an actor who, for fifty years, has made the public laugh and cry without taking his hands out of his pockets! You'll see!"

By the end of the evening, Montgenays had lost his head. Lavallée, without once telling him that he was loved, had given him a thousand hints that he was, and passionately. As soon as Montgenays was clearly trapped, Lavallée pretended to try to undeceive him, but he did it with such clumsiness that the dupe became more and more convinced. Finally, during the fifth act, Lavallée went to see Madame S——.

"Take Pauline home to bed," he told her. "Take the chambermaid with you, and don't send her back to your daughter until fifteen minutes after the play ends. Montgenays must have a tête-à-tête with Laurence in her dressing room. The moment has come: he is ours. I'll be there, hidden behind the full-length mirror. I won't leave your daughter for a moment. Go home and trust me."

Things happened as he had planned, and luck was with him as well. When Laurence entered her dressing room, leaning on Montgenays' arm, and didn't find anyone there (Lavallée was hidden behind the curtain which covered the costumes hanging on the wall, and the mirror hid him from sight as well), she asked where her mother and her friend had gone. A theatre hand who was passing in the hallway answered (and it was unfortunately true) that they had been forced to take Mademoiselle D—— away, because she was having a fit. Laurence was unaware of the scene Lavallée had prepared; in any case, she would have forgotten it as soon as she heard this bad news. Her heart sank; the idea of her friend's suffering, added to the fatigue and intense emotion of the evening, caused her to sink onto a chair and burst into tears. At that very moment the arrogant Montgenays, believing himself to be the master and tormentor of these two women, abandoned all caution, and ventured the most confused and calculatedly delirious declaration that he had ever made. He claimed that Laurence was the woman he had always loved; that only she could prevent him from killing himself or committing an even more horrible act: a moral suicide, a spiteful marriage. He had tried everything to overcome a passion he did not think was shared: he had thrown himself into society, into the arts, into art criticism, into solitude, into a new love; but nothing had worked. Pauline was beautiful enough to be admired; but he couldn't feel anything more than cold respect for Pauline, as long as Laurence was there beside her. He knew very well that Laurence scorned him, and in despair and in order not to hurt Pauline by misleading her any longer, he was going to leave forever!

While announcing this humble resolution, he boldly seized Laurence's hand, but she tore it away in horror. For an instant, she became so indignant that she almost silenced him; but Lavallée, who wanted her to have real proof, slipped to the door, which he had purposely covered with a curtain, apparently draped there by chance. He pretended to arrive, knocked, coughed and entered abruptly. With a glance, he restrained the actress's justifiable anger, and, as Montgenays was cursing him, he managed to lead him away before he had a chance to observe the effect he had produced. The chambermaid arrived and, while she was dressing her mistress, Lavallée returned quickly to tell Laurence everything that had happened. He told her to pretend to be sick and to refuse to see Montgenays the next day. Then he went back to Montgenays and took him home, where he stayed with him till morning, exciting him, and amusing himself with the romantic fictions he spun out for him with comic seriousness. He did not leave Montgenays' house until he had convinced him to write to Laurence; at noon, he returned and asked to read the letter that Montgenays, in the throes of delirious insomnia, had already written and rewritten a hundred times. The actor pretended to find it too timid, too vague.

"You can be sure," he claimed, "that Laurence will have doubts about you for a long time to come; your fancy for Pauline has doubtless inspired misgivings about you that you will have a hard time overcoming. You know how proud women are; you must give up the provincial girl and clearly express how little she means to you. You can manage it without lacking gallantry. Say that Pauline is like an angel, but that a woman like Laurence is more than an angel; say what you say so well in your short stories and skits. Go ahead, and don't waste any time; who knows what may transpire between those two women? Laurence is a romantic, she has the sublime instincts of a tragic empress. A generous impulse, a remaining fear, might inspire her to sacrifice herself to her rival. . . . Reassure her completely, and, if she loves you as I believe she does, as I am firmly convinced she does, even though she has never confided in me, I can promise you that the pleasure of triumph will silence her scruples."

Montgenays hesitated, scribbled madly, tore up the letter, began it again . . . and Lavallée carried it to Laurence.

⋄ VII ⋄

An entire week passed, during which Montgenays was refused entry to Laurence's house and during which he dared not ask Lavallée to explain her silence or her refusal, so great was his shame at perhaps having made a fool of himself, and his fear of having it confirmed.

Behind closed doors, Pauline and Laurence were in the throes of emotional storms of their own. Laurence had tried everything to make her friend admit her feelings, but without success. The more she tried to make Pauline dislike Montgenays, the more she aggravated Pauline's wounds without bringing on the crisis necessary for her salvation. Pauline was angered by these efforts to tear out her heart's secret. She had seen Laurence's attempts to make Montgenays betray himself, and she had interpreted them as he had. Thus she bitterly resented her friend for having succeeded in robbing her of the devotion of a man whom, until recently, she had believed to be sincere. She attributed Laurence's conduct to an odious ambition to have every man at her feet. Pauline thought: "She needed to attract even the one who was the most indifferent to her, as soon as she saw his interest in me. I became the object of her scorn and hatred as soon as she suspected that I had been favored over her, if only by one man. Thus her indiscreet inquiries and her spying to find out what was happening between us; and all the efforts she's making now to keep him from seeing me; and finally, the odious victory she has won through seductiveness, and her easy triumph over me by arousing a weak man who is dazzled by her fame and weary of my depression."

Pauline didn't want to accuse Montgenays of a crime greater than involuntary infatuation. Too proud to pursue an unreciprocated love, she now suffered only the humiliation of having been abandoned; but this was in fact the greatest slight she could feel. She was not a tender soul; anger wreaked greater havoc within her than regret. She possessed enough noble instinct to act and think nobly in the midst of the misunderstanding she was led to by her wounded pride. So although she believed that Laurence had acted hatefully towards her, which was in itself a deplorably ungrateful thought, she didn't want to be ungrateful. Pauline consoled herself by imagining herself better than her rival and by vowing to leave the field open to her, without meanness or resentment. "Let Laurence have her way," she told herself, "let her triumph, that's fine with me. I can resign myself to serving as a trophy, provided that, one day, she is obliged to do me justice, to admire my nobility of soul, appreciate my unfailing devotion, and blush at her own treachery! Montgenays, too, will have his eyes opened, and will realize what kind of woman he gave up for the sake of a famous name. He will repent, and it will be too late; I will be avenged by the brilliance of my virtue."

There are people who lack, not nobility of spirit, but simple goodness. It would be a mistake to lump together those who feel a need to harm others and those who do it in spite of themselves, believing in their own righteousness. The latter are the unhappiest: they keep searching for an ideal they cannot find; for it doesn't exist on this earth, and they lack the capacity for love and tenderness that allows us to accept human imperfection. One might say of these people that they are loving and kind only in their dreams.

Pauline had a sense of righteousness and a genuine love of justice; but between theory and practice, there was a veil which clouded her thinking: it was her immense egoism, which nothing had ever contained and which everything, in fact, had enhanced. Her beauty, her intelligence, her admirable conduct towards her mother, her purity of thought and habit, were endlessly there before her like treasures slowly amassed, whose value she had to be reminded of to keep her from envying those of other people. She wanted to *be someone* and the more she pretended to throw herself into the common lot, the more she resisted being put there. It would have been fortunate for her if she could have analysed herself with the clarity that comes from great wisdom or from simple generosity: she would have discovered that her bourgeois virtue was not without blemish, that her Christianity was not always very Christian, that her past acceptance of Laurence was never quite complete, however genuine she imagined it to be. She would have discovered, most of all, a very particular need to live differently from the way she had lived, to develop and express herself. It was a legitimate need, one of the sacred needs of humanity, but there was no reason to make it a virtue, and it is always wrong to deceive yourself in order to improve your self-image. It's only a small step from there to deceiving others about your worth, and Pauline had taken that step long ago. She wasn't able to step back and admit that she was only a mere mortal after having let herself be deified.

Not wanting to give Laurence the pleasure of having humiliated her, she affected the greatest indifference and endured her suffering with stoicism. This calmness, which didn't fool her friend, for she could see Pauline withering away, filled Laurence with terror and despair. She could not bring herself to deliver the final blow by proving Montgenays' shameful infidelity; she preferred to endure the silent accusation that she had seduced him and taken him away. She had refused to accept Montgenays' letter. Lavallée had told her what it said, and she had begged him to keep it sealed at his house in order to use it with Pauline if necessary; but how she wished this letter was addressed to another woman! She was deeply aware that Pauline hated the source of her misfortune more than its perpetrator.

One day, as he was leaving Laurence's house, Lavallée encountered Montgenays, who had just been refused entry for the tenth time. Exasperated beyond measure, he heaped abuse and threats upon the old actor. The latter at first simply shrugged his shoulders; but when he heard Montgenays extend his accusations to Laurence, and, complaining of having been tricked, explode into threats of revenge, Lavallée, who was a kind and righteous man, could no longer contain his indignation. He called Montgenays a scoundrel, and ended by declaring:

"At this very minute, I regret my age more than ever. It seems that white hair is a pretext for not fighting, and you would think that I was taking advantage of that privilege to insult you without fear of reprisal; but you should know that if I were twenty years younger, I would box your ears."

"That threat is enough to prove your cowardice," Montgenays replied, pale with fury, "and I return the insult. If I were twenty years older, I would slap you first."

"Don't push me too far," cried Lavallée, "because I could ignore any remorse or shame and publicly insult you, if you permitted yourself the slightest disparagement of a person whose honor is more dear to me than my own."

Montgenays calmed down once he was home and thought, quite rightfully, that any public revenge would rebound against himself. After careful reflection, he imagined a revenge more awful than any other: he decided to renew, at all costs, his liaison with Pauline, in order to separate her from Laurence. He dreaded the humiliation of two rejections at once. And he feared that after this initial storm, the two women would unite in mocking or despising him. He preferred to seduce and abandon one, in order to frighten and grieve the other.

With this thought, he wrote to Pauline, swearing his eternal love, and protesting the unspeakable plots that, according to him, Lavallée and Laurence had contrived against them. He requested an opportunity to explain himself and promised never to approach her again if she didn't find him completely justified after their meeting. It had to be kept secret, since Laurence was determined to keep them apart. Pauline went to meet him: both her pride and her love needed to be consoled.

Lavallée, who observed everything that went on in the house, intercepted Montgenays' message. He passed it on, resolved not to abandon Pauline to this wicked scheme, and, from that moment on, didn't let her out of his sight; he followed her when she went out at night, alone, on foot, for the first time in her life, and with such trembling that she nearly fainted at every step. At the first street corner, he appeared before her and offered his arm. Pauline, thinking she was being accosted by a stranger, screamed, and tried to flee.

"Don't be afraid, my poor child," Lavallée reassured her in a fatherly tone, "but look at the risk you're taking going out alone at night like this. Come, then," he added, taking Pauline's arm under his, "if you want to do something foolish; then at least do it properly. I will take you myself; I know where you're going, I won't lose sight of you. I won't hear anything, the two of you can talk, I'll keep my distance, and then I'll take you home. Just remember that, if Montgenays suspects my presence, or if you try to move out of sight, I'll jump on him and flog him with my cane."

Pauline did not try to deny her scheme. She was thunderstruck by Lavallée's self-confidence; unable to explain her conduct and preferring any humiliation to that of being betrayed by her lover, numb and distracted, she let Lavallée lead her to the Parc Monceaux, where Montgenays was waiting in one of the pathways. The actor hid among the trees and kept an eye on her while Pauline, mindful of his warning, strolled back and forth with Montgenays without leaving his sight and without explaining to her lover why she adamantly refused to walk any further. He attributed her insistence to bourgeois prudishness which he thought ridiculous, since he was not foolish enough to begin with any sudden advance. He adopted a serious countenance, a low voice, a discourse full of emotion and respect. He soon realized that Pauline was not aware of either the unfortunate declaration or the embarrassing letter; and from that moment on, it was easy for him to thwart Laurence's plan. He pretended to feel a deep remorse and to have summoned a firm resolve; he devised a new tale, confessing a former passion for Laurence, which he had never dared to admit to Pauline, and which rekindled itself from time to time against his will, even when he found himself at the feet of this delightful girl, so pure, so sweet, so humble and so superior to that proud actress. He had yielded to blatant seduction and frenzied advances; and, recently, had even been foolish enough, acting against his own dignity, his own happiness, to send a letter to Laurence that he now disavowed and detested, but that he wanted to reveal in detail to Pauline. He recited the letter word for word, emphasizing the most damaging, least forgivable passages. He claimed that he didn't want her mercy and would submit to her wrath or her banishment, but that he couldn't bear her scorn.

"Laurence will never show you the letter," he said; "she has worked too hard at winning me back to give you such proof of her flirtatiousness; so I didn't have anything to fear of that sort; but I didn't want to lose you without letting you know that I humbly submit to your judgment, with repentance and despair. I wanted you to know that I take back my letter, and I'm asking you to deliver a new one to Laurence. You'll see how I judge her, how I treat her, how I despise her! This cold, haughty woman, who never loved me and who wanted to be eternally adored! She has ruined my life, not only because she thwarted all the hopes she offered me, but because she prevented me from wooing you as I should have, as I could have, as I still might, if you can forgive my cowardice, my crime, my folly. Torn between two loves, one stormy, devouring and deadly, the other pure, spiritual and enlivening, I betrayed the one that would have nurtured my soul for the one that is destroying it. I am a wretch but not a scoundrel. Just consider me a weak man overcome by the long suffering of a deplorable passion; know, too, that I will not survive my remorse: only your pardon could have saved me. I can't implore it for I know I don't deserve it. You see me at peace, because I know I won't suffer long. Don't be afraid to accord me a little pity; you will soon hear that I did you justice. You have been insulted and you need someone to avenge you. I'm at fault and I will be your avenger."

For two whole hours, Montgenays carried on in this manner with Pauline. She dissolved into tears; forgave him, promised to forget everything, begged him not to kill himself, forbade him to go away, and promised to see him again, even if it meant breaking with Laurence. Montgenays hadn't expected as much, and didn't ask for more.

Lavallée walked her home. She didn't utter a word the entire way. Her silence did not surprise the old actor; he had supposed that Montgenays would find fine phrases and solid lies to calm her. He thought that she was lost unless he took dramatic action. Before leaving her at Laurence's doorstep, he slid Montgenays' first letter, still sealed, into her pocket.

Laurence was very surprised that night when she saw Pauline enter her bedroom at bedtime, seemingly calm and affectionate—Pauline who for the last week, had been consistently curt and ironic. She was holding a letter which she handed to her, saying that it had been given to her by Lavallée. When Laurence recognized Montgenays' seal and handwriting, she thought that Lavallée must have had a good reason to entrust Pauline with this message, and that the moment had come to apply a strong remedy to a serious problem. She opened the letter with a trembling hand, glanced at it, still unsure whether to show it to her friend, for fear of hurting her terribly. She was stupefied when she read the following:

"Laurence, I have misled you; it is not you I love, it is Pauline; don't blame me, I fooled myself. Everything I told you was true at the time; but now and forever after, I disown what I said. It is your friend whom I adore and to whom I would like to devote my life, if she can forget my folly and hesitation. You have tried to lead me astray, to seduce me, to make me believe that you could and would make me happy; you wouldn't have succeeded, because you don't love me, and I need true, deep and lasting affection. Forgive my weakness as I forgive your capriciousness. You're extraordinary, but you're a woman; I'm sincere, but I'm a man; we almost made a serious mistake, we almost misled each other, but we have reflected and changed our minds, haven't we? I'm now ready to place at the feet of your friend my life's devotion, and you have resolved to let me woo her in earnest, if she doesn't reject me. Be assured that by behaving frankly and nobly, you will find in me a faithful and trustworthy friend."

Laurence was dumbfounded: she couldn't get over such impudence. She put the letter in her desk without revealing her surprise. But Pauline thought she could read her soul, and resented the evil intentions she attributed to her friend.

"I was given the letter insulting me," she told herself on her way to her bedroom; "here is one that might console me, and she doesn't share it with me." She fell asleep full of contempt for her friend; and the joy that flooded her soul was so filled with pleasure at finding herself superior to Laurence, after all, that she felt no regret at the friendship betrayed. The wretched girl gloated, unaware that she had just participated, with malice, in bringing about her own ruin.

The following day, Laurence discussed the letter at length with Lavallée. Chance or custom caused it to be absolutely identical, in its fold and seal, to the one that Montgenays had written under Lavallée's watchful eye. They asked Pauline whether she hadn't had two identical letters in her pocket when she handed this one to Laurence. Jubilant at their disappointment, she feigned surprise, pretended not to understand the question, not to know the source of the letter, nor why or how it had been slipped into her pocket. She had already returned the other to Montgenays. In her extravagant joy, Pauline, wanting to offer him a grand romantic sign of her trust and pardon, had returned the letter to him without opening it.

Laurence still wanted to believe in a sort of loyalty on Montgenays' part. But Lavallée couldn't be mistaken. He told her about the rendezvous to which he had led Pauline and reproached himself for it. He had counted on the fact that after a meeting where Montgenays lied openly, the letter's effect on Pauline would be decisive. He could not yet understand how Pauline had been so ready to help Montgenays triumph perversely over all obstacles. Laurence refused to believe that Pauline herself had known about the intrigue and had played such an undignified role in it.

What could Laurence do? She made a last attempt to open her friend's eyes. Pauline unleashed her anger at last, and, refusing to believe any other explanation than that offered by Montgenays, she tore at Laurence's heart with her bitter reproaches and triumphant deluded disdain. Laurence felt obliged to issue a few stern warnings, which only exasperated Pauline. And when Pauline declared that she was independent, of age, free to do as she pleased, and not at all inclined to be bound by the arbitrary whims of someone who had shamelessly misled her, Laurence was forced to tell her that she wouldn't be a party to her ruin, and that she would never forgive herself for having allowed a seducer and a coward to venture into her home, among her family.

"I am responsible for you before God and man," she said. "If you wish to throw yourself into the abyss, I'm not going to push you into it myself."

"That explains why your devotion went so far," quipped Pauline, "as to try to throw yourself there in my place."

Shocked by such injustice and ingratitude, Laurence stood up, gave Pauline a terrible look and, afraid to express the wave of anger that rose within her, she showed her the door with a gesture and an expression that terrified Pauline. The actress had never been so beautiful, even when, in *Bajazet,* she ejaculated her imperious and magnificent "*Get out!*"

Once alone, Laurence paced her bedroom like a lioness in a cage, breaking Etruscan vases and statuettes, crumpling her clothes, and tearing at her beautiful black hair. All the grandeur, sincerity and genuine tenderness in her soul had just been misinterpreted and vilified by the one she had loved so deeply, and for whom she would have given her life! There are sacred angers when Jehovah is within us, when the earth would tremble if it felt what happened in a heart grievously offended. Laurence's younger sister came in, thought that she was rehearsing a part, watched her for a moment without a word, without daring to move; then, terrified at seeing her so pale and so furious, she went to tell Madame S—:

"Mama, come and see Laurence; she's going to get sick from working so hard. She frightens me."

Madame S— ran to her daughter. As soon as Laurence saw her, she flew into her arms and burst into tears. After an hour she calmed down and asked her mother to fetch Pauline. She wanted to apologize for her violent reaction and have a chance to forgive Pauline in turn. They looked for Pauline everywhere— in the house, in the garden, in the street. They came back to her room in great fright. Laurence searched everywhere, she looked for traces of an escape; she feared finding those of a suicide. She was in a state impossible to describe, when Lavallée came in and told her that he had just seen Pauline in a coach on the boulevard. They anxiously awaited her return; she did not come back for supper. No one could eat; the family was dismayed; they were afraid of insulting Pauline by assuming that she had run away. Finally, Lavallée was about to go to Montgenays to ask about her, at the risk of an angry scene, when Laurence received the following letter:

"You have driven me out, and I am grateful to you. My stay in your house has been unbearable to me for a long time. I felt, from the first day, that it would be deadly to me. Too many storms and scandals have taken place there for a peaceful, honest soul not to be tarnished and battered by it. You have degraded me long enough! You made me your servant, your dupe, and your victim! I will never forget the day at the theatre, in your dressing room, when I wasn't dressing you fast enough to suit you and you tore your queen's crown from my hands, crying: 'I will crown myself without you and in spite of you!' And indeed, you crowned yourself! My tears, my humiliation, my shame, my disgrace (for you have disgraced me within your family and among your friends), were the glorious spikes of your crown; but it's only theatrical majesty, false grandeur, that deceives and inspires you and the public who pays you. Now I bid you farewell; I'm leaving you forever, haunted by the shame of having lived on your charity; I have paid for it dearly. . . ."

• • •

Laurence didn't read the end of the letter; it went on in this vein for four pages: Pauline had poured out all the bitterness that had slowly accumulated over four years of rivalry and jealousy. Laurence crumpled the letter in her hand and threw it into the fire without wanting to read any more. She felt feverish when she went to bed and stayed there for a week, overcome, shattered to her very core: she had loved Pauline as a daughter and a sister.

Pauline had retired to a garret, where she lived for a few months in hiding, eking out a miserable living with her labor. Montgenays found her quickly; he saw her every day, but could not easily overcome her reticence. She preferred to live like a pauper rather than to be in his debt. She rejected in horror the gifts that Laurence managed to slip into her garret through the most ingenious means. Nothing worked. Pauline, who refused Montgenays' offers with calm and dignity, recognized those from Laurence with an instinct born from hatred, and sent them back with heroic pride. She refused to see her, although Laurence tried a thousand times; Pauline returned all her letters unopened. Her resentment remained unshakable, and Laurence's generous solicitude only renewed her strength.

Since she didn't really love Montgenays, and had only wanted to triumph over Laurence by attracting him, this heartless man, who wanted to take her as a mistress or get rid of her, tried to offer her a deal. She threw him out. But he led her to believe that Laurence had pardoned him, and that he was going back to her. She immediately called him back and that is how he kept her under his thumb for another six months. He was himself becoming attached to her because of the difficulty of overcoming her virtue; but he succeeded at last through despicable means, completely consistent with his methods, and particularly apt to move Pauline. He disciplined himself to repeat to her several times a day that Laurence had become virtuous by design, in order to marry a rich and powerful man. Laurence's blameless life during the past several years had often created in Pauline, in her weak moments, a feeling of resentment. She would have wished her friend to be more dissolute, so that she could have felt dazzlingly superior to her. But Montgenays managed to make Pauline see things in a new light. He was determined to convince her that by refusing herself to him, she was lowering herself to Laurence's level; her tactic had been to make herself desirable in order to win a husband. He made her believe that by abandoning herself to him with devotion and without remorse, she would be giving the world a great example of passion, unselfishness and magnanimity. He repeated this so often that the wretched girl came to believe him. In order to behave differently from Laurence, who was the most generous and passionate soul, Pauline performed acts of passion and generosity, she who was both cold and cautious. She plunged to her ruin.

When Montgenays had made her pregnant, and the whole affair had been widely and publicly discussed, he married her ostentatiously. He had, as you know, pretended to be an eccentric with moral principles, although he claimed that his great success and seductive power with women turned him into a rake. He attracted as much attention to the affair as he could. He spoke ill of Laurence, Pauline and himself, let himself be accused and blamed constantly, in order to create a great effect when he gave his name and fortune to his love-child.

Thus this trite tale ended in marriage, and that was Pauline's greatest misfortune. Montgenays no longer loved her, if he ever had. He played the role of an admirable husband before society, and then left his wife crying backstage while he went about his business, or his pleasure, without remembering that she even existed. Never was a vainer woman, or one more hungry for glory, left more abandoned, humiliated, and obscure. She saw Laurence again, hoping to make her suffer by showing off her happiness. Laurence was not deceived, but she spared Pauline the pain of her knowledge. She forgave Pauline everything, forgot all her wrongs, and was touched only by her suffering. Pauline could never forgive Laurence for having been loved by Montgenays, and remained jealous of her for the rest of her life.

Many virtues derive from negative qualities. We shouldn't have less respect for these virtues because of that. The rose doesn't create itself, but its perfume is no less sweet when it emanates from it unconsciously; we mustn't wonder that the rose wilts in the space of a single day, or that great domestic virtues wither quickly on a stage they were not designed for.

Notes

1   See Rousseau's *Julie ou la Nouvelle Heloise* (1761), in which the protagonist refuses to be treated as a servant by his hosts. See this theme also in Stendhal's *The Red and the Black* (1830).

2   Marie Rainteau, the actress Mademoiselle de Verrière, was the mother of Marie-Aurore de Saxe and thus George Sand's great-grandmother.

3   Abraham-Joseph Bénard (1750–1822), known as Fleury, joined the Comédie Française in 1778, playing aristocrats and libertines, most especially in the plays of Mauvaux.

4   *Andromaque* (1667) is a tragedy by Racine.

• Selected Bibliography •

Barry, Joseph A. *Infamous Woman: The Life of George Sand.* Garden City, N.Y.: Doubleday, 1976.

Manifold, Gay. *George Sand's Theater Career.* Ann Arbor: UMI. Research Press, 1985.

Naginski, Isabelle: *George Sand. Writing for Her Life.* New Brunswick: Rutgers University Press, 1991.

Powell, David A. *George Sand.* Boston: Twayne, 1990.

Rogers, Nancy: "George Sand: Social Protest in Her Early Works" *George Sand Papers: Conference Proceedings, 1976.* New York: AMS Press, 1980, 66–91.

Sand, George. *Correspondance.* Ed. Georges Lubin. 25 volumes. Paris: Garnier Frères, 1964–91.

———. *Gabriel.* Paris: Des Femmes, 1988. (Also in translation, by Gay Manifold)

———. *Nouvelles.* Paris: Michel Lévy, 1861. (First Edition).

———. *Nouvelles.* Paris: Des Femmes, 1986. Excellent introductions (omits *Melchior*).

———. *Story of My Life.* Albany: State University Press of New York, 1991.

Schor, Naomi: *George Sand and Idealism.* New York: Columbia University Press, 1993.

Winegarten, Renée. *The Double Life of George Sand: Woman and Writer.* New York: Basic Books, 1978.

Witkin, Sylvie Charron: "Les *Nouvelles* de George Sand: fictions de l'étrangère." *Nineteenth Century French Studies* 23, 3/4, 1995, 365–72.

———. "*Eugénie Grandet* et *Pauline:* optiques romanesques chez Balzac et Sand." *George Sand et l'écriture du roman*, ed. J. Goldin. U. de Montréal: Paragraphes, 1996, 389–97.